Penguin Book 2166

KU-425-161

The Pumpkin Eater

Penelope Mortimer was born in North Wales and studied at London University. Her first writing consisted, in her own words, of 'poetry and short stories of immense gloom and obscurity'. After the war she reviewed novels for *Our Time* and had one or two articles published in the *New Statesman*. She also wrote a script for the B.B.C. and an occasional documentary-film commentary. Her first novel was published in 1947 and *The Pumpkin Eater* is her seventh published book. Penelope Mortimer, who is married to the playwright John Mortimer, is also widely known as a critic and for her short stories, most of which have appeared in the *New Yorker*. She has six children and lives in London.

Penelope Mortimer

The Pumpkin Eater

Penguin Books

by arrangement with Hutchinson of London

Penguin Books Ltd, Harmondsworth,
Middlesex, England
Penguin Books Pty Ltd,
Ringwood, Victoria, Australia

First published by Hutchinson 1962
Published in Penguin Books 1964
Reprinted 1964

Made and printed in Great Britain by
C. Nicholls & Company Ltd
Set in Linotype Granjon

For John

Peter, Peter, pumpkin eater,
Had a wife and couldn't keep her.
He put her in a pumpkin shell
And there he kept her very well.

I

'Well,' I said, 'I will try. I honestly will try to be honest with you, although I suppose really what you're more interested in is my not being honest, if you see what I mean.'

The doctor smiled slightly.

'When I was a child my mother had a wool drawer. It was the bottom drawer in a chest in the dining-room and she kept every scrap of wool she had in it. You know, bits from years ago, jumpers she'd knitted me when I was two. Some of the bits were only a few inches long. Well, this drawer was filled with wool, all colours, and whenever it was a wet afternoon she used to make me tidy her wool drawer. It's perfectly obvious why I tell you this. There was no point in tidying the drawer. The wool was quite useless. You couldn't have knitted a tea-cosy out of that wool, I mean without enormous patience. She just made me sort it out for something to do, like they make prisoners dig holes and fill them up again. You do see what I mean, don't you?'

'You would like to be something useful,' he said sadly. 'Like a tea-cosy.'

'It can't be as easy as that.'

'Oh no. It's not at all easy. But there are other things you can make from wool.'

'Such as?'

'Hot water bottle covers,' he said promptly.

'We don't use hot water bottles. Balls you can make, for babies. Or small golliwogs.'

'The point you are trying to make is that tidying the wool is a useless and probably impossible task?'

'Yes.'

'But you are a human being. The consequences of your ... muddle are more grave. The comparison, you see, is not a true one.'

'Well, it's how it feels to me,' I said.

'When you cry, is that how it feels? Hopeless?'

'I just want to open my mouth and cry. I want to cry, and not think.'

'But you can't cry for the rest of your life.'

'No.'

'You can't worry for the rest of your life.'

'No.'

'What do you worry *about*, Mrs Armitage?'

'Dust,' I said.

'I'm sorry?'

'Dust. You know? Dust.'

'Oh,' he said, and wrote for a while on a long piece of paper. Then he sat back, folded his hands and said, 'Tell me about it.'

'It's very simple. Jake is rich. He makes about £50,000 a year, I suppose you'd call that rich. But everything is covered with dust.'

'Please go on.'

'It's partly the demolition, of course. They're pulling down the houses all round us, so you have to expect a bit of dust. My father bought the lease of the house for us when we got married, that was thirteen years ago.'

'You have been married for thirteen years,' he said, writing it down.

'To Jake, yes. There were thirteen years of the lease to run when my father bought it. He bought it for £1,500 and we pay a peppercorn rent, so you see we're lucky. Anyway. I was trying to tell you about the dust.'

'So your lease expires this year.'

'I suppose so. We're building a tower in the country at the moment.'

'A tower?'

8

'Yes.'

'You mean . . . a house?'

'No. A tower. Well, I suppose you could call it a house. It's a tower, though.'

He put his pen down carefully, with both hands, as though it were fragile. 'And where is this . . . tower?' he asked.

'In the country,' I said.

'I realize that, but – '

'It's on a hill, and down in the valley is a barn, where I used to live before I married Jake. That's where we met. Now can we get back to the dust, because . . .'

'Of course,' he said, and picked up his pen again.

I tried to think. I stared at him, silhouetted against the net-curtained window of the consulting-room. I heard the tick of the clock, the hiss of the gas fire. 'I've forgotten what I was going to say.'

He waited. The clock ticked. I stared at the fire.

'Jake doesn't want any more children,' I said.

'Do you like children, Mrs Armitage?'

'How can I answer such a question?'

'Could it be a question that you don't wish to answer?'

'I thought I was supposed to lie on a couch and you wouldn't say a word. It's like the Inquisition or something. Are you trying to make me feel I'm wrong? Because I do that for myself.'

'Do you think it would be wrong not to like children?'

'I don't know. Yes. Yes, I think so.'

'Why?'

'Because children don't do you any harm.'

'Not directly, perhaps. But indirectly . . .'

'Perhaps you don't have any,' I said.

'Oh, yes. Three. Two boys and a girl.'

'How old are they?'

'Sixteen, fourteen and ten.'

'And do you like them?'

'Most of the time.'

'Well, then. That's my answer. I like them most of the time.'

'But you have ...' He glanced at his list and made do with, 'a remarkable number. You seem upset that your husband doesn't want any more. This hardly sounds like someone who likes children most of the time. It sounds more of ...'

'An obsession?'

'I wouldn't use that word. Conviction, perhaps, would be nearer the mark.'

'I thought I was meant to lie on a couch and talk about whatever came into my head.'

'I'm not an analyst, Mrs Armitage. I simply want to find out how you should be treated.'

'Treated for what?'

'We don't know yet, do we?'

'For wanting another child? Is that why Jake made me come to you? Does he want you to persuade me not to have another child?'

'I am not here to persuade you of anything. You came of your own free will.'

'In that case I do everything of my own free will. Crying, worrying about the dust. Even having children. But you don't believe that, do you?'

'I'm not here to believe you, Mrs Armitage. That isn't the point.'

'You keep saying you're not here to do this, that, and the other. What *are* you here for?'

'Perhaps,' he gave another of his wan smiles, 'to find out why you hate me so much, at the moment. Oh, I don't mean myself, personally, of course. But you hate something, don't you ... other than dust?'

'Doesn't everyone?'

'What was the first thing you hated – can you remember?'

'It wasn't a thing. It was a man. Mr Simpkin ...'

'Yes?'

'And a girl called ... Ireen Douthwaite, when I was a child. And a woman called Philpot. I don't remember ...'

'Your previous husbands?'

'Oh no. No. I liked them.'

'Your present husband? ... Jake?'

'No!'

'Tell me about Jake.'

'Tell you ...?'

'Yes. Go on. Tell me about Jake.' He sounded as though he were daring me. I laughed and spread my hands out, looking down on them.

'Well, what ... what do you want to know?'

'Whatever you want to tell me.'

'Well, Jake ... It's impossible to tell you about Jake.'

'Try.'

I took a deep breath. I felt as though I could open my mouth and pour words out for ever. I felt as though I could open my heart, literally unlock it and fling it open. Now the truth would be told. The breath petered out of me. I said nothing. He waited.

'This house we live in,' I began. 'The sitting-room faces south, it has huge windows, sash windows, so whenever there is any sun it's like a greenhouse, very hot indeed. Of course the sun shows up the dust. When people come into the sitting-room for the first time they always say what a marvellous room it is, and then after a bit I see them noticing things. Women mostly, of course, but also men. Somebody once wrote an article about Jake; they said he bought books, not yachts. Well, of course, he doesn't buy either. He doesn't buy anything. The things people notice are the burns in the carpet and the marks on the wall. Jake used to drink a lot of tinned beer, and you know how it spurts out when you make a hole in the tin. Then the children. Well, nobody has ever washed the walls, for some reason, I mean not since it was last painted, about two years ago.

'Of course it is a marvellous room. I'm in there most of the time now, I really live in it. I do know it very well. There's a picture on the side wall, here, just as you come in the door, a terrible yellow and green thing, an abstract. It belongs to Jake. We don't get rid of it, although it's the most hellish picture you've ever seen. There are piles of magazines, too. We don't get rid of things. We've still got bicycles in the shed that we brought from the country years ago. Quite useless. Then there's nowhere to put the new ones.

'Anyway. Jake has a study downstairs, he used to work there a lot until he got this office. His office is in St James's, that's where he works now. I haven't been there for a long time. He never liked working in the study at home, he used to feel lonely. He was always coming upstairs to talk to someone, the children, or me, or whoever was in the house. He used to cook things for himself, he was always hungry, he liked being in the kitchen. Of course Jake was an only child. We both were. There are eight bedrooms, but we've only got one bathroom. I don't know what else to tell you.'

There was a long silence. I thought he might have gone to sleep. That gas fire would send anybody to sleep; he ought to have a bowl of water in front of it.

'Shall I go on?'

'Please.'

'Isn't it time to stop?'

'Only if you want to.'

'You ought to have a bowl of water in front of that gas fire, you know.'

'You find it too hot?'

'The trouble is that people throw their match ends into it and they float about for days. Then the water dries up.'

'You hate . . . messes, don't you?'

'Yes. That is something I hate.'

'They frighten you.'

'Perhaps they do frighten me.'

'Was . . .' he glanced down at his paper, 'Mr Simpkin a mess?'

'Yes,' I said. 'To me he seemed the most terrible mess. Is that helpful?'

He stood up, leaning on his desk like an after-dinner speaker. 'We shall, I think, make progress,' he said.

2

Jake's father said, 'I suppose you know what you're doing. What do the children say?'

'They – '

'We haven't actually *discussed* it with them,' Jake said. 'They are *children*, you know. We don't have to ask their permission, do we?'

'Indeed,' his father said, 'I should have thought that was most important.'

'I don't understand why you want to marry Jake,' he went on, delicately biting the end off a cheese straw. 'Simply don't understand it.' He smiled in my direction, holding the straw poised for the next bite.

'I know there are an awful lot of us, but – '

'Oh, I'm not worrying about that, not worrying about that at all. I suppose your previous husbands pay a bit of maintenance and so on?'

'A little,' I lied.

'You've managed so far. I should think from the look of you you'll go on managing. Why Jake, though? He'll be a frightful husband.'

'Now wait a minute – ' Jake said.

'Oh, he will. A frightful husband. You're bound to be ill, for instance. You won't get the slightest sympathy from him, he hates illness. He's got no money and he's bone-lazy. Also he drinks too much.' He smiled very sweetly at Jake, congratulating him.

'You'd think he hates me,' Jake said.

'Nonsense, my dear boy. She knows better than that. Give her some more sherry, but don't have another Scotch, it's got to last me till Tuesday. Now where are you going to live, for instance?'

'We don't know yet ...'

'Well, it's entirely your own affair of course. If I were nicely settled in a house in the country with furniture – I presume you've got furniture – and all the usual amenities, I certainly shouldn't abandon it all for Jake. He's totally unreliable, always has been. And I wasn't even aware that he liked children. Do you,' he inquired blandly of Jake, 'like children?'

'Of course. I'm mad about children. Always have been.'

'Really? How strange. Now I would have thought you would have found them tremendously boring. Have you *known* many children?'

'You see?' Jake said. 'I told you. He's impossible.'

'You're not drinking all my Scotch, are you?'

'I'll get you another bottle.'

'Where? It's Thursday, you know, early closing.'

'I'll go down to the pub before lunch and get you another bottle. All right?'

'You will see that he does, won't you?' the old man asked me. 'He *plunders* me, you know. The last time he was here he walked off with my razor –'

'For heaven's sake,' Jake said, 'you had *six* razors.'

'I need six razors. I hope you brought it back.'

'No. I didn't.'

'Perhaps you could send it me, my dear? It's a small Gillette, the kind that screws open, I believe they cost around five and elevenpence.'

'I'll see if I can find it,' I said. 'Otherwise, of course, we'll buy you a new one.'

'That would be kind. It's a quite indispensable little razor for getting at the odd corners, you know. Now, Jake, stop mooning about, boy. Give her some more sherry. His manners aren't up to much, but I expect you've discovered that already.'

'Actually,' I said, screwing up my toes, my voice squeaking a little. 'Actually, I love him.'

'I'm sure you do. So do I.'

We smiled warmly at each other.

'You're a brave girl,' he said.

'Oh, no. It's Jake who's ... brave.'

'Nonsense. He's out for what he can get. Beautiful wife who knows how to cook, ready-made family, plenty of furniture. He'll expect a lot of you.'

I reached for Jake's hand. 'I don't mind.'

'He's been on his own too much. My wife couldn't have any more children, we spoiled him. He doesn't like his shirts sent to the laundry, you know that?'

'Good God,' Jake said. 'I'm twenty-nine years old. I am *here*.'

'He also has a shocking temper. When do you plan to get married?'

'Next month,' I muttered. 'When the divorce is through.'

'Ah, the divorce. That's all going smoothly?'

'I think so. I'm sorry that Jake – '

'He's the co-respondent, of course. "All experience is an arch wherethro' gleams that untravelled world ..." I must say, dear boy, I never thought you had it in you. Well ... that's everything, I think? We needn't go on with this discussion, need we? How about getting my Scotch?'

'I hope you'll come,' I said. 'I mean, we'd like you to be there, if you'd like to come.'

'Oh, I don't think so. Thank you, my dear, but I don't think so. I detest trains, and if I get Williams to drive me up we can never park anywhere, and then there's the problem of Williams's lunch. No, it's all too tedious. But of course you have my great blessing.'

'As far as the wedding present's concerned,' Jake said, 'we'd like a cheque.' His face was a very delicate green and his upper lip was curled under in a petrified flinch.

'A cheque,' the old man said. He became motionless. A shaft of sunlight moved idly over the room, picking out little pieces of silver and cut glass, lighting up the old man's polished toecaps, sliding over the leather chairs. He took another cheese straw, weighed it in his fingers. 'What for?'

We couldn't answer that. He waited, then bit the straw neatly. 'I'll give you a cheque. Not much, mind you, because I'm a poor man. You'll want a little party, I daresay, after the event, a few bottles of champagne and so on. I'll give you twenty-five pounds on the express condition that you spend it on that. You understand me?'

'But we *can't* – ' I began.

He looked at me sharply for the first time. 'On second thoughts,' he said. 'Get a caterer. And send me the bill.'

*

My father said, 'There are a few quite practical points I'd like to get straight. Sit down, Armitage. Can I roll you a cigarette?'

'No, thanks,' Jake said. He lowered himself on to a battered leather pouf patterned in dark blue and red diamonds. My father swivelled himself round to his desk and adjusted the lamp to shine exactly over it. 'Are you pouring the tea, dear?' he asked.

'Tea?' I asked Jake. We had just had sausages and mash and banana custard for supper.

'No. No, thanks.'

'There's some elderberry wine in the larder,' my father said. 'Darling, run and get the elderberry wine.'

'No, thanks,' Jake said. 'Really.'

'Well, then. We'll declare the meeting open.' He swivelled round again and smiled encouragingly at Jake. 'Now we don't want to go into the whys and wherefores of all this. You're both grown people, with minds of your own. I must say that for a young man with his life in front of him to saddle himself with a brood of children and a wife as plain feckless as this daughter of mine seems to me lunacy. Lunacy. The only good thing about it is that at last she's picked a *man* and not some ... fiddler or scribbler like the others. I like you, Armitage. I think you're a fool, but I'd like to help you make a go of it. You think that's fair?'

'Thanks. Thanks very much,' Jake said. 'Very fair.'

'If I give you a start, you think you can carry on from there?'

'I hope so.'

'I hope so too. The first thing is to shed the load a bit. I suggest we send the elder children to boarding school. I have particulars of a couple of schools here, perhaps you'd like to look them over?'

He handed two leaflets to Jake and sat back, tapping his pencil on the edge of the desk. 'They're only a few miles apart,' he said. 'Both by the sea. Of course they're not Harrow or Roedean exactly, but it'll give them a chance of getting scholarships later on, if they're bright enough. What do you think?'

'No,' I said. 'Of course not. We can't send them away, they're too young. Anyway, we can't afford it. Anyway – !'

'Pipe down, dear,' my father said tartly. 'This is Jake's business, not yours. I'm taking out educational policies that will pay for their schooling for the next five years. That will make them respectively ...' he glanced at a sheet of paper on his desk, 'fourteen, twelve, and eleven. We should know by then whether they're capable of getting any further, and Jake will have had a chance to get established. What do you think?' he asked Jake.

'I think it's a very good idea.'

'No!' I said.

'Look, be sensible,' Jake said. 'They'd love it. It'd be good for them.'

'It wouldn't! They'd hate it! Why can't you just give us the money – ?'

'Because that's not the point,' my father snapped. 'I'm not going to have you crushing this boy with responsibility from the word go. As it is he's taking on far more than he can chew, and he's got to work like a nigger to do it. I don't know anything about this ... cinema business, and I haven't got much faith in it, to tell you the truth. But I'm not going to have you trailing home with half a dozen more children in five years' time and another messed-up marriage on your hands. I'm sorry to be so blunt, but that's the size of it. It's high time you saw a little sense, my girl.'

He had never before spoken to me like this. 'Jake – ' I said, 'Jake – ?'

'Your father's quite right,' Jake said. 'It'd make things a lot easier.'

They sat there unmoved, looking at me.

'Anyway ... what about the holidays? They'd have holidays.'

'They can come here,' my father said. 'Your mother loves having them, as you know.'

'You mean ... they're just going to go away. For ever. That's what you mean, isn't it? Why don't we get them adopted, or something? Why don't we *give* them away?'

My father sighed deeply and turned back to his desk. 'You'd better work this out between you,' he said. 'The offer stands, that's all I can say. Now ... the next point. Where are you going to live?'

'It'll have to be in the country,' Jake said.

'You can't work from the country?'

'At the moment I can. Later I may have to get a room or something ...'

'That's no good,' my father said. 'A man needs regular meals, someone to look after things. There's no point in *making* difficulties for yourself, is there? You've got enough without that.'

'I don't quite see the alternative, sir.' The 'sir' was astounding. Changed already from the man I had always known, my father suddenly seemed to grow vast, threatening, absolutely powerful.

'We've always lived in the country,' I said, but neither of them listened to me.

'A good friend of mine happens to be an estate agent,' my father said. 'He has a link-up with a firm in London. It seems there's a lot of new planning going on and it's possible to buy a fairly short lease on one of these old houses for quite a reasonable sum. Here's one, for instance. Have a look at it. It'll pretty well clean me out, mind you, but I'd sooner you had it now, while you need it, than wait until I'm dead.'

'I don't know why you should – '

'If I'd had a son,' my father said, 'I'd have known how to bring him up. No problem. We failed with this girl here. There's no question of it, we failed. It's time she had a firm hand on her tiller, and I've got a strong notion that you're the chap to put it there.'

'I'm *here*!' I said. 'Why can't you talk to *me*?'

My father leant over and patted Jake's shoulder. 'Good luck,' he said. 'Good luck, my boy, you need it.'

After the wedding, we had a party. The caterers brought small chicken sandwiches, trifle, and champagne. Everyone was very happy. My mother cried, as usual, and my father clasped Jake's hand, speechless, as though he were about to take off into orbit. The children, who were being looked after for the day by my mother's Mrs Norris, sent us Greetings telegrams. A fortnight later the three eldest went to boarding school.

We moved into the house my father had found for us, and the surviving children came up by train. They had a great deal of luggage, for I insisted that they brought everything : clothes and sticks, toys, pots, Malt, books, diaries, horseshoes, conkers, ribbon and string and a shedful of punctured bicycles. They invaded the local schools, where they were known collectively as the Armitages, so that for convenience and solidarity those who had post office savings books or sent up coupons for silver-plated teaspoons or entered competitions for winning ponies, changed their names; and those who were too small had theirs changed for them and grew up used to the idea that in any list, roll call or census they came very near the top.

Only the three at boarding school remained apart, cut adrift, growing old under their old names. They were my first children, and although they had always been gloomy and hard to please I felt desolate without them. I burned with anger, but dully. Anger against whom, against what? It was all for the best, that boy and those girls set on the right path, flannelled and stockinged for Jesus and the General Certificate of Education, stripped for ball games in the bitter cold. It was right for Jake that they should go. Slowly, little by little, almost imperceptibly, I let them drift until only our fingertips were touching, then reaching, then finding nothing. Our hands dropped and we turned away. The younger children always felt kindly towards them, the three melancholy Conservatives who grew to hate Jake with such inflexible devotion. In time, they included me in this hate. They were my first enemies. My mother sent them each ten shillings at the beginning of every term, fastened to the letters with small gold safety pins.

With Jake's child I went to hospital for the first time. Jake was thirty and beginning to worry about his hair. He was deprived, nervous, over-excited. He was working on his first full-length script, and he told me that one day he would build a tower of brick and glass overlooking the valley where we met.

3

'I don't know what's the matter with me,' Philpot said. 'Sometimes I shake all over and sometimes I have a temperature of ninety-three. Sometimes I cry for hours on end.'

'Why don't you see a doctor?'

'They'd just say it was the worry. I mean, there's nothing you can do about worry, is there?'

'Well,' I said, 'I don't know ...' I was cleaning out the kitchen cupboards, a sign of unease. The girl – she was in fact a woman of twenty-four whose surname was Philpot – had said she was sure there was something she could do. I had set her to cleaning saucepan lids with steel wool. She did it slowly, sitting on the edge of the sink and stroking the dented lids round and round as though they were faces.

I took the new Coronation mugs off the shelf, a clutch in each hand, and put them on the floor. Then I asked Philpot to move so that I could get some more hot water. She heaved herself up on to the fridge and spread her skirt over it.

'Goodness,' she said, 'what a lot of mugs. Poppy was given one too. Aren't they rather divine . . .'

'I think they're hideous,' I said. 'But we've got dozens of spoons.'

'Yes,' she said, 'Poppy got a spoon too.' She looked out of the window to the garden, where some of the younger children and Poppy were sitting each in an individual cardboard box doing, as far as I could see, absolutely nothing. She sighed gustily. 'I wonder if there'll ever be another Coronation. I mean, while we're alive.'

'Oh, sure to be.' I felt she needed reassuring. 'Why? Did you like this one?'

'I did indeed. Such wonderful parties. Poppy went to stay with my aunt.' I scraped bits of butter off six saucers on to a plate, and moved her off the fridge. She settled like a great duck on the cooker. 'And I had a simply wonderful time, although I slept all through the actual thing on TV. Shall I hand you the mugs, or something?'

'No,' I said. 'It's all right.'

'Well, of course, it all ended in disaster. It always does with me. People's wives get so ratty somehow. And I mean, I *like* them, that's the funny thing. I like them really better than their husbands. Sometimes I wonder if I'm quite normal. I mean, I *have* been told I'm frigid, but I don't see how you can tell. I mean, honestly – how can you tell?'

'I shouldn't think you are,' I said. 'Could I get to the oven?'

'I'm in your way, I know I am. I'm sure there's something I could do. I feel useless, and you working away like a black.'

'Anyway, you don't look frigid,' I said, peering with some despair into the greasy cavern of the oven. 'And you can't say fairer than that.'

'It does me so much good to talk to you,' she said distantly. 'It's marvellous to talk to someone who *knows*. I really can't think how you manage, I mean with so little help and all those children. Of course Jake's a perfectly gorgeous father, I can see that. Poppy's mad about him. Well, of course, having no father she's mad about any man, poor little sweet, but she's especially mad about Jake. I do wish I had half your luck, although of course I know it's not luck really, you're so intelligent and attractive and capable and everything, you deserve every bit of it.' There was a long pause. Being partly inside the oven I could only imagine the wistful blue eye and the pinkish strand of hair that she nervously pulled down over it. 'But oh crumbs,' she said, 'I do envy you.'

I don't remember how we came to meet Philpot, but at that time we knew many minor characters in the film world, and she must have been attached to one of them. I liked her because she was lonely and eccentric and kept making little rushes at life which were, as she swore she had always known, doomed to failure. Perhaps, in a way, I envied her too. She was like girls at school who had brothers, but no love.

Every day, that summer, she turned up and mooned about our house, pushing her little awkward child into the garden and staying indoors herself, drinking in great draughts of what she called family life. She was tremendously anxious not to disturb Jake, but would tiptoe past his study door leaving such a smell of gardenia behind her that in a few moments he would come out, sniffing, and join us in the kitchen or the sitting-room cluttered with patterns and pins, for we took to dress-making at that time. There he would sprawl on the sofa and hold me with one arm while Philpot asked him about his work. She knew every detail of the film he was writing. Every day she would ask after the characters as though some mishap beyond Jake's control might have befallen them in the night. She wore striped blouses and large skirts and usually clenched her collar with some sort of cameo brooch – she had a weakness for cameos, china hands and boots, paper weights, stuffed birds and velvet photograph frames. Occasionally she would go away for a couple of days with someone who happened to be driving to Exmoor or Cardiff or Leeds. Then we would take over Poppy, though without joy, since none of us liked her very much. She made the boys feel foolish by prodding them, and bored the girls with inaccurate descriptions of love.

4

'Why does Philpot have to stay with us?' they asked.

'She's been turned out of her flat.'

'But why does she have to stay with us? We've got enough people.'

'She's looking for another one.'

'I've never seen her looking. She just stays in bed all the time if you ask me.'

'In *my* bed, too. Why can't she bring her own bed? I'm not going to sleep in that awful cot again.'

'It's a perfectly good cot.'

'It's not, and I'm not going to sleep in it.'

'Look, there's a squirrel.'

'I'm not going to sleep in that cot.'

'Where's Poppy?'

'Poppy's staying with her aunt.'

'Then why can't Philpot stay with her aunt?'

'Because Philpot's aunt lives in Gloucestershire and Philpot can't look for a flat, I mean couldn't look for a flat if she was in Gloucestershire.'

'She could come in a helicopter.'

'I'm not going to sleep in that cot.'

'I'm glad Poppy's in Australia.'

'Must you wade in the puddles? You don't have to wade in them.'

'Well, I wish she'd go home, that's all.'

'She can't. She hasn't got a home.'

'She smells of fish.'

'No, she doesn't. She smells like roses rather.'

'She smells like roses and fish, but fish most.'

'I'm not going to sleep in that awful cot.'

'She had a spot on her chin yesterday, but this morning she'd squeezed it. Don't tell Dad, he'd say change the conversation.'

'He had to grab her yesterday, when she fainted. It must have been awful for him, the smell.'

'Fainted?'

'She fainted when you were out for your walk.'

'Do you faint like this? Is this how you faint?'

'Oh, for heaven's sake, get up! You're smothered in mud, it'll take me hours to brush it off, hours!'

'I was only asking.'

'I'm not going to sleep in that ...'

We were spread out over a quarter of a mile of Heath; converging, in a brown, sodden afternoon, on Dinah playing netball. Why should anxiety touch me? I looked across to one of London's unexpected hills, topped with a broken steeple. Fly away home, your house is on fire. The older children, in shrunken blue duffel coats, ran pell-mell down the slope and leapt on my back. Jake's children stamped and fell down in the wet leaves.

'I can see them,' I said, and we stumbled down into a desolate slum patch of ground scattered with a few corrugated iron sheds. Various children in short-sleeved cotton jumpers and long skirts and gumboots were festooned about a great bare tree, while others made vague motions with a football in the wet grass that someone had tried to mark out with chalk. 'Where's Dinah?'

We found her shivering in the corner of the field, holding her stomach and saying she had a terrible pain. She looked at us with envy; even, it seemed to me, with affection. The mistress, a young, quite pleasant-looking woman sensibly dressed in a leather coat, called 'Dinah!' with the rising inflection, tinged with strain, that women use towards children at the end of a hard day. Dinah shuffled off, and the mistress pushed them all into a ragged circle and attempted to show them something. The damp, darkening afternoon was quiet except for their incessant coughing. They began to lollop about, throwing the ball with feeble gestures, from hip-level. 'Keep moving!' the mistress exhorted them. 'I'm going to stir you up like a pudding!' She ran amongst them, darting heavily to and fro while the children fell in the mud and held their stomachs and gazed into the foggy distance.

'Can we go now?'

'I'm cold, I'm freezing.'

'I'm not going to sleep in that cot.'

'Then run about. Run about and get warm.'

'Why should I? I'm tired.'

'Why do we have to come and see Dinah play football?'

'I'm *tired* ...'

A girl in baggy tartan trousers, a windcheater and a fur hat came slowly over the brow of the hill. For a moment I thought she was Philpot. She dragged a pram after her and stopped, kicking the wheels viciously because they were stuck up with mud. Then, after looking down on us for a few moments, she went back the way she had come. As she was submerged, first pram and finally hat, I was irrationally convinced that she had come to give me some message from the outside world; but that like a rescue craft she had looked, seen nothing, and gone home.

5

'Is Philpot given to fainting much?'

'Fainting?'

'The children said ...'

'Well? What? What did they say?'

'They said she fainted yesterday.'

'Oh. Well. Perhaps she did.'

'They said you were there. That you caught her.'

'Caught her when she fainted?'

'Yes.'

'Why should I catch her when she faints?'

'I don't know. But did she?'

'I don't know! I don't remember!'

'There's no need to shout.'

'Shout? My God, it's not me who's shouting.'

The incessant company of children leads to this kind of dialogue: it was our mother-tongue, incomprehensible to most adults, and in it we carried on the complex, subtle and occasionally tragic conversations which are the last resort of communication between men and women. Jake, although he had learned the language comparatively late in life, had a more perceptive ear and a more imitative nature than I. He was particularly expert at the intonation and the repartee. Now he said, after a moment's thought, 'It's you who's shouting.'

I looked at him as carefully as I dared over the magazine I had been pretending to read. Since that afternoon, six or seven hours ago, I had felt a very curious sensation. It was like being petrified in the moment of falling: the heart had frozen in its leap, blood thrown out of its course, muscles rigid, throat dry with the onslaught of air. It seemed to me that I was frightened, but I was not sure.

It was midnight. Jake had turned the electric fire on when

we came in from the cinema, but the curtains were undrawn. Philpot had left the sitting-room door open when she went.

'Where has she gone?' I asked.

'How should I know.'

'It seems very peculiar.'

'What does?'

'Well, to come to the pictures and then just ... go like that.'

'It's none of our business what she does.'

'Oh no,' I said, 'it's none of our business certainly.'

I stared at the magazine. Jake lay in the armchair with his overcoat on. We trembled like dogs before a storm. High up in the house beds made little whining noises.

'But,' I said, 'she's left all her things.'

He didn't answer. I thought of Philpot's bedroom in our house: the layers of grime-edged broderie anglaise flung over the unmade bed, the spilled powder, little stumps of lipstick and unstoppered deodorants. I thought how in the afternoon one ray of sunlight, if it was a fine day, shone through the small attic window, and how the child who was now asleep in a resented cot grumbled incessantly about the loneliness, the darkness of that room, and said nobody would hear if it died. I thought of how at ten o'clock that morning I had taken Philpot breakfast in bed, partly because the knowledge of her sleeping so tirelessly had irritated me, but partly because Philpot was a poor girl who had no one to love her, and made such a mess of life and wasn't strong and competent and in command of the situation like myself. I thought of myself strongly and competently and commandingly creeping across the heaths and parks of London every afternoon, returning home to find Philpot freshly pinned and painted saying oh damn, I really, honestly, meant to get the tea. I thought of Philpot leaving us so quietly, as though she were sacrificing herself that we might survive: eyes a little puffy, but with a great air of nobility about her, now I came to think of it, as she waved her lace handkerchief at us from the door and said good-bye. I looked up at Jake.

Possibly fifteen seconds had gone by, but during that time, under cover, as it were, of these inconclusive thoughts about poor Philpot, some of my innocence, trust, stupidity, idealism, had been stripped away from me like skins. I was smaller, uglier, more powerful than I had been before, and I felt bewitched by fear.

'What happened between you and . . . Philpot?'

'Happened? What d'you mean – happened? Nothing happened.'

'Then why did she suddenly leave like that?'

'I've told you I don't – '

'And you weren't surprised. Were you? You knew she was going.'

'Leave it alone, can't you? Leave it alone.'

But he did not get up, change the conversation. He hunched further into his overcoat, staring at me over the upturned collar. It was the steadiness of this stare, not its expression, that was melancholy. I looked at his eyes. They might have been made of glass. They were empty. They moved as I moved, watching me get up, walk up the room, back again, sit down on the sofa.

'You were holding her hand in the cinema,' I said. 'How extraordinary.'

'What's extraordinary?'

'That I knew you were. Perhaps I actually saw you were. But I didn't believe it.'

'It's not a crime, for God's sake.'

'But you were holding mine as well. Keeping us both happy.'

'What the hell does it matter whose hand I was holding?'

The tremendous beats of my heart began to shake my body and my voice. I said, 'Oh, it doesn't. It's quite . . . unimportant.'

'Well, then.'

'Except that you don't usually hold somebody's hand unless you, unless you want to . . .'

But I couldn't go on. Dignity, please, a little dignity, this is the most foolish way to behave, short-sighted way to deal with what is after all the most common ...

'It was a mere peccadillo,' Jake said abruptly, as though about to recite.

'What?'

'Peccadillo. Bagatelle.'

'I don't understand.'

'It doesn't matter.' He yawned, so widely and for so long that it seemed he must dislocate his jaw. For a full half minute I looked at his back teeth and palate and quivering tonsils. His face, when he composed it, seemed rested. 'I love you. So why worry?'

'Did you ask her to leave?'

'Oh lord, no. That was her idea.'

'Why?'

'I don't know. She thought you might·be ... upset or something.'

'Why should I be?'

'Oh, for Christ's sake, don't you *understand*?'

'No, I don't understand.'

'Well, then ...' He got up, stood with his hands in his pockets and his head slightly on one side, smiling at me. 'Well, then, I can't help you, can I?'

I stared at him. After some time, a few moments perhaps, he turned away and said, 'Look, I can't see what you're so horrified about. I've told you it was nothing. Hell, I don't want to *leave* you. I don't want to *marry* the girl.'

'That's to comfort me?'

'You haven't exactly been a model of faithfulness yourself, you know.'

'I was never unfaithful to anyone. To anyone. Ever.'

'You really believe that? God, what a bloody hypocrite you are – '

'But you say it's *nothing*. You keep saying it's nothing. Why bother, then? Why hurt people so much, for what you say is nothing?'

'Why do you feel so hurt?'

'Because I care about you! I care!'

'About *me*? You don't give a damn for me, and you know it. Shut up! You don't care about *me*, all you care about is the bills being paid and the bloody children, that great fucking army of children that I'm supposed to support and work my guts out for, so I can't even take a bath in peace, I can't eat a bloody meal without them whining and slobbering all over the table, I can't even go to bed with you without one of them comes barging in in the middle. If you cared about me you'd try to understand me, wouldn't you? All right, I'm a bastard! All right, I'm no good to you! But what joy do you think *I* get out of this god-awful boring family life of yours? Where do *I* come in?'

He was shouting as though I were a mile away. His shouts delighted me. I forgot Philpot. I loved him. He was yelling and bawling like a man being delivered of devils.

'What the hell are you sniggering at? It's funny when *I* tell the truth for once, I suppose? The truth is something strictly reserved for you, isn't it? Well, let me tell you, my sweet, you live in a bloody dream world. You wouldn't know what the truth was if it stared you in the face!'

'I think I would,' I said. 'It is now.'

'Yes. It is now. But you don't know what it is, do you?'

'What is it, then?'

'That I'm capable of fancying someone else. That I'm a perfectly normal man who can fancy someone else.'

'I'd forgotten about Philpot,' I said.

'Good. Then what the hell are we arguing about?'

'I don't know. Nothing. I suppose it's just ... nothing.'

I got up from the sofa and walked slowly towards the door. I knew that I wouldn't leave him, that I was not going out of the room, but I had to move somewhere. He said, 'You're going to bed now, I suppose.'

'No. Just shutting the door. In case the children hear you shouting.'

'Give me a drink, then. I'm not going to shout any more.'

As I handed him the drink he caught me and pulled me on to his knee. For a few moments he held me tightly, an awkward, dead armful.

'I didn't mean any of that,' he said. 'I'm sorry.'

'Any of what?'

'About the children. I love the children, you know that.'

'You were telling the truth.'

'Was I?'

'I think so.'

'You do see how it was, don't you?'

'You mean about Philpot?'

'Well, she was here. I know it wasn't very noble of me, or anything like that. I just felt fed up. Bored to death with this script. You did rather hand her to me on a plate, didn't you?'

'I didn't think of it.'

'No. Well, you wouldn't, I suppose.'

He craned up to kiss me. Like a child, with puckered mouth and closed eyes, he waited. I looked at him carefully. I thought of my other husbands, decent, adult, unselfish men from whom I had escaped while escaping from my childhood – each one an insufficient parent, readily left alone. They seemed to watch me while Jake waited for his maternal kiss. Now it's your turn to suffer, my girl. Now it's up to you to do the forgiving and forgetting. Now it's your turn to refuse freedom or give it out inch by inch.

'You didn't tell me,' I said. 'But I suppose you slept with her?'

He did not open his eyes, but shook his head violently.

'You didn't?'

'No. Of course not. Now kiss me, forget it.'

'You promise me?'

'I promise. I promise.'

I bent warily and kissed him. He was filled with the urgency and excitement of a man released from danger.

'But do you still want to?' I asked, merciless.

'Not if I don't see her again.' He smiled up at me. His eyes were still quite empty, and I realized now that they never changed, even in love. 'You won't let me see her again, will you?'

'No,' I said.

For an instant, before he reached again, he looked puzzled.

*

I took every string and jar and puff and rubber band and hair clip of Philpot's, every velvet ribbon and safety pin, every packet and box, full or empty, every piece of her clothing down to the laddered stockings in the wastepaper basket and I tied them up in her genuine Victorian shawl with black braid round the edges and dumped them in the front garden. It was a fine, warm night. The roses were at their best in the moonlight, when you couldn't see how blackened and blighted they were. I took her sewing machine and dressmaker's dummy and portable wireless and a terrible lemon and green abstract that Jake had once offered to buy, and piled them neatly beside the dustbins. Then I sat on the front steps and probed the sensation of fear, which after all that running up and down stairs had dulled to a slight physical pain, as precisely located and bearable as mild toothache.

What, I asked myself, was I frightened of? Thirty-one years old, healthy and whole, married to a fourth husband (why four?) who loved me, with a bodyguard of children (why so many?) – what was I frightened of?

Not of Philpot, surely? Oh no, not in the slightest of Philpot. Of whom, then? Of what?

I soon began to feel cold. Unused to long, solitary bouts of thinking, I remarked to myself that I was cold and therefore got up and went indoors. It occurred to me that there was probably some etiquette for this situation which I didn't know. Perhaps I ought to sleep somewhere else. There was nowhere else to sleep, except in Philpot's bed. I didn't consider it. I walked about the house for a while. The younger children were already shifting about, rolling their heads from side to side and muttering. The one in the cot had thrown all its bedclothes on the floor and was so wet that it appeared to be drowned, not sleeping. Dinah opened her eyes and said, 'There's the most awful smell in this room,' and shut her eyes and slept on.

At last I went into the bedroom, undressed and got in beside Jake. In his sleep he looked puzzled again. I thought of waking him up, but for the first time I could not touch him. This paralysis, this failure of my will to make my body move, revived all my fear, and I lay there sweating, shaken by great beats of my heart, ignorant as in a first labour but with no instinct, or memory to help me. It must have been then, I think, that Jake and life became confused in my mind, and inseparable. The sleeping man was no longer accessible, no longer lovable. He increased monstrously, became the sky, the earth, the enemy, the unknown. It was Jake I was frightened of; Jake who terrified me; Jake who in the end would survive. He rolled over, his mouth slightly open, and began to snore.

6

'Most enviable New Year resolution comes from writer/producer Jake Armitage, whose latest who-done-it mirth-jerker, *The Sphinx*, starts shooting mid-January. Jake's plans? To say "No" at least once a week to movie moguls who are out-bidding each other to buy his services. "I'm a yes-man by nature," says Jake, "but there comes a point when you've got to sit back and live a little." Jake, now one of the highest paid scribblers in the business, started ten years ago on a re-write of a B-picture weepy for Lazlos Rothenstein, since when he has never looked back.

'Beth Conway, John Hurst and Italian discovery Maria Dante are three of the stars of *The Sphinx*, the new comedy-thriller which Jake Armitage has scripted and will produce for Tower Productions.

Doug Wainwright directs, and locations will be shot in North Africa.

'I congratulated Mrs Armitage on running her large household with such apparent ease. "It wasn't so easy once," she said, laughing. "There was a time when we didn't dare to answer the door in case it was someone coming to sue us!" Those days are far away now, for since that first £100 script, taken on to keep the wolf from the door, the Armitages have never looked back ...'

*

Everything is silent in the afternoon. Everything keeps still. The Jag is out of the garage, but the Floride is in. The grass will be mown when it starts to grow. The dishes are clean in the dishwasher and the rubbish eater has eaten the rubbish away. A Froebel-trained girl with a good complexion and a hard heart sits resting in her room. She writes to her friends and smokes one of her two daily Turkish cigarettes with a cup of weak tea. Soon she will let herself out of the front door and walk energetically from place to place, collecting the children from schools.

There: the latch clicked: she has gone. I could dust the room or tidy the magazines now the house is empty. But why? It's somebody else's job. Somebody else never does a job properly. The food is tasteless. There's no incense of furniture polish about the rooms as there used to be. The toys are never sorted out and Jake has gone to lunch with two buttons missing from his shirt. It's somebody else's job. Why can't somebody else do a job properly? Heaven knows we pay them enough.

Jake has been at lunch for four hours. His secretary doesn't know where he is. She smirks at me over the telephone. Oh, there's such treachery. Stop punishing me, God.

It is the afternoon and I have nothing to do. I'll go and buy something for Dinah, to protect her: a possession, to protect her. A petticoat, a pair of stockings. The Oxford Companion to French Literature. When I was fourteen I had the world at my feet but somebody didn't do their job properly and allowed me to sin. They are not getting on with the building of the tower, they are not doing it right. I have told them a hundred times, but they are incapable of building a simple tower even at that price.

Yesterday – I remember it so well – everything was all right. Tomorrow, what with superlative tax at 18s. 6d. in the pound and the companies I am married to – Mrs Production Limited is my name, I spring from an Armitage Enterprise – tomorrow everything will be different. But today? Today I am a legitimate expense. I direct without the faintest sense of direction; I share and have nothing to hold. At least I make myself laugh. When I walk round the shops and never decide to buy, I am looking for something to buy, but there is nothing to buy.

What did I come here for? Why did I walk, in the spring, along a mile of pavement? Do I want a bed rest, a barbecue, a clock like a plate or a satin stole or a pepper mill or a dozen Irish linen tea towels printed, most beautifully, with the months of the year? April brings the primrose sweet, scatters daisies at our feet. I am beginning to cry. I stand in the bloody great linen department and cry and cry quite soundlessly, sprinkling the stiff cloths with extraordinarily large tears. Oh, what has happened to you, Mrs Enterprise, dear? Are your productions limited, your trusts faithless, and what of the company you keep? Think of all those lovely children, dear, and don't cry as the world turns round holding you on its shoulder like a mouse.

But I cried just the same. The doctor they sent me to was expensive and Jake said, 'Do you think you're going to get over this period of your life, because I find it awfully depressing?'

7

It was late at night and all the children, even Dinah, were asleep. Jake had just gone downstairs with our family doctor, a sturdy, middle-aged G.P. who had never seen me ill before, although he had bullied and encouraged me through many labours. He had given me an injection earlier in the evening, but when I woke up the tears were still pouring out, a kind of haemorrhage of grief. Now, exhausted, I wondered if I was going out of my mind. Was this how it began, with this terrible sense of loss, as though everyone had died?

I got out of bed and went to the door; it squeaked when I opened it, but the landing light wasn't on, so I ran to the banisters and leant over. As I had hoped, the sitting-room door was open. I couldn't hear what they were saying, so I crept half-way down the stairs. Now I could hear. I crouched on the stairs, hugging my knees, alert for the sound of the nurse or a child but straining for every word through the open door.

'... very unhappy,' the doctor said.

'What did she say to you?'

'Nothing very much. Why? Do you think ...?'

They were moving about the room. I heard the hiss of the soda syphon. '... gets mad ideas into her head,' Jake said.

'What sort of ideas?'

'Oh ... thinks everyone's against her, finds fault all the time. You know the sort of thing.'

'I've known it in many people, not your wife. Don't forget I've known her for, what is it, eleven, twelve years. She's a remarkable ...' He must be leaning forward for his drink. 'Tough, sensible, full of life. This doesn't make sense to me.'

'Doesn't make sense to me, either.'

'No, I don't, thanks ... She's not got enough to do, you know.'

'Oh, balls ... Sorry, but that's a lot of balls. She never sews on a button, never lifts a duster, never cooks a meal ...'

'Since when?'

'I don't know. The last few months. Just sits here and mopes all the time.'

There was a short silence. I eased myself farther down the stairs. My heart was pounding again and I felt sick. Eavesdroppers, my mother would say, hear what they deserve.

'How are you getting on? Together, I mean?'

'Oh ... fine. I'm busy, of course. But ... fine.'

'So you can't think of any reason for this ... sudden collapse? She's very disturbed, you know. I don't think you should take it lightly.'

Why didn't Jake speak? 'Jake!' I had cried, 'Jake!', as the crackling white nurses had carried me off for aspirin and sweet tea in some kind of antiseptic rest room through Lingerie. 'Jake! Jake!', as though I were literally dying of grief. But they hadn't been able to find him, so one of them had brought me back in a taxi, allowing me to hold her plump, grey-gloved hand, and the children, just back from school, had stared dumbfounded as I was helped upstairs.

'No,' Jake said. 'I can't think of a reason ...' The syphon hissed again. 'I suppose ... she'd like to have another child.'

'How old is she?'

'I don't know. Thirty-eight, I think.'

'And the youngest?'

'Three.'

'Then why doesn't she have one? When this little storm's over, probably just the thing. She drops those babies like a cat, you know – it's a pleasure to watch ...'

'We've got enough children! Good God, we've got enough!' The doctor murmured something I couldn't hear. I was shivering. 'It may be a pleasure to watch for *you* ... When's she going to face facts? She can't go on having children for ever, anyway what *for*? They'll all grow up in the end. She's got a bloody houseful already, and me, she's got me! Why can't she grow up, settle for what she's got, why can't she take some interest in the outside world for a change? I'm sick of living in a bloody nursery! ...' There was a long silence. He must have paced to the far side of the room because I could hardly hear him now. '... her ... all right ... can't go on indefinite ... *obsession* ...'

'Obsession is a very strong word,' the doctor said.

'All right. It's a strong word.' Jake came to the doorway, his back to me. He had one hand in his pocket and the other hammered his words. 'Look, I work harder than anyone else in the business. I work because I like working, and because I like money. Right. But all she wants is to sit in some shack with a tin of corned beef and have more *children*. Is that sane? She's got everything any woman could want – clothes, a car, servants, she's attractive. Why doesn't she go abroad, or make some friends or ... make a life for herself? That's what I don't understand.'

'Maybe she doesn't want to,' the doctor said.

Jake stalked away out of sight. 'You're dead right she doesn't want to. Drink?'

'No, thanks. I must be going.' I heard the effort of raising himself from the sofa and got up, ready to run. 'I see your point, Armitage. But has she ever said to you that she wants another child?'

'Not in so many words. No.'

'She didn't say so to me, either. I wonder ... if you're right?'

'I don't know. I give up.'

'I shouldn't do that ... just at the moment.'

'I get back to the office after a bloody hard day and I'm told my wife's gone off her nut in Harrods. Harrods, of all places. Well ... what do we do?'

'I think she should probably see a psychiatrist, try and get this depression sorted out before it takes root, you understand. I know a very good man ... You'd like to pay, of course? You don't want this on the National Health?'

'I suppose so. I mean, yes. I'll pay.'

'There's a lot you can do in the meanwhile. I hope you will.'

'Such as?'

'Be kind to her, for a start.'

'I'm always kind to her.'

'Tell her ... well, you know. Tell her you love her and so forth.'

'I never stop. But it's not me she wants. I've told you. It's another bloody baby she wants.'

'I should cut down on the drink, if I were you. It doesn't ... it doesn't help the situation.'

'It helps me.'

'Yes. Well. Your wife loves you, you know.' He was coming towards the door. I ran, two stairs at a time, to the landing. This was the place, hidden by the linen cupboard, where children peered down at parties. My teeth were chattering. I pressed my hands over my mouth. 'I'll come again in the morning. You have the tablets, but don't give her any more unless she starts weeping.'

They walked slowly along the hall. Jake's scalp shone pink through his dark, thin hair; the doctor had grey hair like a mat.

'Perhaps she ought to go away?' Jake said.

'Could you go with her?'

'I'm afraid not. I'm off to North Africa in a couple of weeks and I've got a hell of a lot to get through before then.'

'Why not take her to North Africa?'

'She wouldn't want to go.'

'Are you sure of that?'

'I've asked her. She hates going on location. You know, there's nothing for her to do, she just sits about and gets in the – she feels she gets in the way.'

'I see. Well ... take care of her. I'll see you tomorrow.'

'I've got one or two things I must do, so if I'm not here I'll ring you. All right? I'll ring you at lunch time.'

'I should stay here if you can,' the doctor said.

I drew back quickly. The front door slammed. I turned to race to the bedroom, but Jake wasn't coming upstairs. He had gone back into the sitting-room. The telephone dial whirred deliberately, seven times. He began to speak, but so softly that I couldn't hear a word. I waited for a few minutes, but it was a long conversation. I got into bed and lay down flat under the bedclothes. At last I heard the sharp ting as he put down the receiver. Now he was having another drink. Now, heavily, he was coming up the stairs. I closed my eyes. He opened the door very cautiously.

'Asleep?'

'No ...' I held out my hand. He took it, sitting on the edge of the bed. 'Has he gone?'

'Yes. Don't wake up.'

'What did he say?'

'Oh ... nothing much.' He bent over and kissed my forehead. 'We'll straighten you out. Don't worry.'

'When will they finish the tower?'

'Soon. Go to sleep now. Happy dreams ...'

I shut my eyes. He stroked my hair for a time, until he grew uncomfortable; then he went away.

A woman whom I knew to be his mother closed the door. We were in a dark castle. She was going to have a party, she said; we were invited. We were there early, eating a meal with Jake's mother and another woman who didn't like her very much. She said, 'I've asked Philpot for a cup of tea.' There was a storm and we ran for shelter, Jake and myself and the others, I was wearing a fur coat. Philpot was standing wearing terrible clothes, looking plain and poor. The party began. There were hundreds of people in a vast, white, icy hall. 'Who are these people?' I asked, 'and why don't we know them too?' Someone said, 'They are Jake's cousins.' Jake wasn't there and I was nervous, but there was a Paul Jones, so I joined in and danced with the Mongol boy. It was a marvellous dance, elated, soaring. I was enjoying it, but he went away and I walked over to a group of street-corner louts who were sitting on a bench and asked, 'Why don't you dance?' One of them said, 'I don't dance with hard-faced bitches.' I said, 'I'm not a hard-faced bitch,' and he believed me. We waltzed very beautifully on the ice.

I walked down a broad, long corridor, as though dug out of the earth. Philpot was walking a long way in front of me carrying a great sheaf of copper beach leaves. I laughed, unpleasantly, and she dropped the leaves and ran away. When I reached them, the leaves had all disintegrated into dust and twigs. I felt ashamed, and found her in a brightly lit little cabin with her child. 'I'm sorry I laughed,' I said. She burst into tears and threw something at me, something soft, a cushion or a scarf. I caught it and gave it back to her and walked away.

There was a huge barn, and wagons made out of ice. I sat on top of one of the wagons with a lot of other people, waiting for a film to begin. It began, and Philpot, dressed in stuffy clothes and a cartwheel hat, was the Snow Queen. 'She is here in a menial capacity,' I said, 'as an actor.' The lights went out and she sang, off key and rather sadly, a little song. Jake appeared, sitting by me on the wagon. I said, 'I'm having a *wonderful* time, what have you been doing?' He said, 'I've been making love to your friend here.' I looked down, there was a schoolgirl in an old, broken down car beside the wagon.

Jake and I set off somewhere, through a great fair. I kept on saying how much it must have cost. We found that we had to go the wrong way, through a chain of caverns, each cavern contained Mickey Mouse or Popeye or the Sleeping Beauty. But we were going the wrong way. We walked along the truck lines and at last climbed up a conveyor belt: the belt carried wooden painted mermaids, which were going down, but it was not too difficult. When we came out, the party, the people, had all gone: nothing was left but icy water lapping against the walls, darkness and cold. A man in uniform, a fireman, was poking about in the water. Jake had disappeared. I looked and searched, but couldn't see him. Then I heard him calling and saw a hand coming up out of the water. I ran and put my hand down into the water, feeling the rim and neck of some big jar or hole into which he had fallen. I felt his head and hand inside. He was holding a blade of grass and I pulled at it, trying to pull him out, but it broke. I shouted for the fireman, but he shouted back, 'I've got six more down here!' I tried to hold Jake, to pull him out, but my hand kept slipping and at last he stopped moving, and I knew he was dead.

8

'I don't think, at the moment, we need to think in terms of treatment of any sort. Your immediate need, I feel, is for someone to talk to. Say twice a week. Shall we see how we get on?' He was wearing a different suit today, sombre tweed and a heather-mixture tie.

'All right,' I said. 'So long as I can think of something to talk about.'

'Oh, I don't think that will be too difficult.' He slyly uncapped his pen. 'How's the weeping?'

I didn't want to disappoint him. 'Better, I think.'

'We'll give you some tablets to pep you up a little. Children all well?'

'Dinah's got 'flu or something.'

'Dinah. Let me see, Dinah is the ...' Again he raked, worried, down the list. 'She's sixteen,' I said.

'Ah, yes.' He was almost cosy today. 'You must have difficulty finding names for them all.'

'That's what everybody says. It's stupid. There are hundreds of names. My grandmother had fifteen children and each one of them had at least three names. That makes forty-five names if you work it out, but she didn't find it difficult.'

'Your father's mother?'

'No, my mother's mother. Of course a lot of them died.'

'You could hardly hope to keep fifteen children in those days.'

'But you could now.'

'Yes ...' he said slowly; then, darting up at me, 'How's Jake?'

'He's gone to North Africa.'

'Indeed? On location, I suppose.'

If he was trying to be a father to me, he was dreadfully succeeding.

'Yes,' I said. 'On location.'

'Now why didn't you go too?'

'Well, they're living in tents ... you know ... he didn't think I would ... Anyway, I can't leave the children.'

'But you have plenty of staff?'

'Yes, but ... Anyway, I can't leave them.'

'I see.'

He sat back and looked at me gravely. Then, with a short sigh, he glanced down at my file. 'You have had no illnesses? Miscarriages, difficult confinements?'

'No.'

'You have never ... terminated a pregnancy?'

'Of course not. Why should I?'

'But you weren't exactly ... well off before you married Jake? One would have thought that the financial burden ...'

'Look,' I said, 'it was easy. We always lived in the country, and most of the time it was the war. We ate cornflakes and eggs and carrots, things like that, because I didn't know how to cook anything else, so we were vegetarians. I don't mean we were vegetarians because we didn't believe in eating meat, I just didn't know how to *cook* meat. Well, we didn't need any clothes. My mother used to knit things for the children, but the boys and the girls all wore the same clothes because it was easy, and so did I. My second husband, that's Dinah's father, bought dozens of sheets and white cups when we were married, so we were still using those when I married Jake. *What* financial burden?'

'Well, the school fees alone ...'

'There weren't any school fees. They went to the village school. We got free milk and free orange juice – that gummy stuff, we used to drink it with gin when some friend or some-one brought some gin – and we never went out, except some-times to the pictures. That cost ninepence. After the begin-ning we never had to buy cots or prams or nappies, anything like that. It's complete nonsense about this financial burden. It costs a good deal less to keep a child for two years, three years, than it does to have an abortion Why? – Do you think I should have had abortions?'

He blinked several times, picked up his pen and put it down again. 'Of course not,' he muttered valiantly. 'Of course not.'

'Anyway we had a bit of help from my mother.'

'Ah. I see.'

'She hardly ever wrote to me without pinning a ten shilling note to the letter. She used to fiddle the house-keeping money, my father never knew. She always pinned it on with a safety pin, a little gold one, because she didn't think paper clips were safe, and an ordinary pin might have pricked the postman's finger ...' He smiled politely. 'I should think she used to send me a pound a month. It paid for cigarettes, you know, and sometimes toys. The children never ate sweets, I don't know why.'

'It sounds very ... idyllic,' he said.

'No, it wasn't idyllic. But it was all right.'

'You were happy. Or rather, you think now that you were happy.'

'Yes. I mean, I know I was.'

'But you had two divorces, and for a short time you were ... a widow.'

'Yes. But I wasn't unhappy. It's as though ... as though between the time I was a child and the time I married Jake nothing happened. As though everything stopped. I didn't seem to grow any older, I didn't seem to change at all. Then suddenly I was married to Jake and it all started again where it had left off when I was seventeen. But I was twenty-seven then. Do you understand what I mean?'

He wrote rapidly for a full minute. When he had finished

he pondered, fingers steepled under his nose. 'Tell me about your first husband.'

'Oh lord,' I said. 'I can't remember.'

'Can't remember? But you were married to him for ... nearly five years.'

'He was a reporter on our local paper. But the war broke out just after we were married and ...'

'He was in the Forces?'

'No, he was a conscientious objector. They put him on the land.'

'And what happened?'

'Nothing. I had the children and he ... well, he worked on the land.'

'You liked him, you said?'

'Oh, yes. He was sweet. He drank too much, that was the only thing.'

He waited, but I didn't offer him any more information. I couldn't think of any more. At last he was driven to ask, 'And how did it end?'

'It didn't really end. I met the Major – he was Dinah's father – at a sort of ... concert in the village hall. He was a very sober, military sort of schoolmaster, rather intelligent. He read *New Writing*, and *Horizon* and so on. He was a great one for making lists. He was very interested in the children, liked teaching them to read and count beans, you know, things like that. My husband, the first one, was pretty hopeless with children. So we fell in love. I think it was quite a relief, really, divorcing me – for my husband, I mean. He cried a good deal at one point, but it was only the drink.'

There was a long pause.

'And then?' he asked coldly.

'Then? Well, then I married the Major, but since he was going overseas we went back to live with my parents. I had Dinah there. Of course he was dead by then.'

'And did that upset you?'

'Yes. Yes, I suppose it did. Naturally. It must have done.'

He slumped in his chair. He seemed tired out. I said, 'Look, need we go on with this? I find it tremendously boring, and it's not what I'm thinking about at all. I just don't think about those husbands except ...'

'Except when?'

'I never think about them.'

'We're almost at the end.' The smile had grown even weaker. 'I'm sorry if it's painful for you, but it helps to know the facts. Who was the next one?'

'Giles. He was a professional violinist. I suppose he still is. He came with some quintet to play chamber music in the Town Hall, something to do with C.E.M.A. or E.N.S.A. or one of those things. Anyway, the Major had left me £200 in his will and Giles seemed to think he could manage the children. I don't think I ever loved anyone in the way I loved Giles – except maybe a boy once, when I was very young.'

'Then ...'

'Why? I don't know.'

'Was it something to do with the children?'

'I don't know. I can't remember.'

'Did you insist on having children – which he didn't want?'

'No! He loved children!'

'Why did it go wrong, then? What happened?'

'Nothing happened! I've told you, that was the thing about that time – nothing happened!'

'And yet after four years you were ready to leave ... Giles and marry Jake. Something must have happened.'

'I just had to go on, that's all! When I stopped wanting ...'

'Wanting?'

'To go to bed with him. Then there was nothing. No future. Nothing to look ...'

'But why did you stop wanting to go to bed with him? Because he didn't want any more children, and sex without children was unthinkable to you, a kind of obscenity? As it is with Jake, now? Isn't that true?'

'No! It's not true!'

'Don't you think sex without children is a bit messy, Mrs Armitage? Come now. You're an intelligent woman. Be honest. Don't you think that the people you most fear are disgusting to you, and hateful, because they are doing something for its own sake, for the mere pleasure of it? Something which you must sanctify, as it were, by incessant reproduction? Could it be that in spite of what might be called a very full life, it's sex you really hate? Sex itself you are frightened of? What do you think?'

'You really should have been an Inquisitor,' I said. 'Do I burn now, or later?'

He laughed heartily. 'I'm glad to see your sense of humour flourishing.' Everything about his face, except the jovial mouth, was as cold as mine. 'Now, I was going to give you a prescription, wasn't I?' The pen flourished again. 'One twice a day ... There you are. I think they'll deal with those little weeps of yours. But keep them away from the children.'

'Yes,' I said. 'Thank you, doctor.'

'And don't be down-hearted. Great progress is being made. Great, great progress.'

9

Although he has no use for Freud ('all that cock'), Jake would unhesitatingly say that I longed all my life for a husband like my father: practical, positive, a man with a work bench, reliable. But then, my father was not like this. His reliability was invented by Jake. My father was a complete provincial. His ideas sprang directly from his own actions, and his actions were necessary to the way he lived. Nothing from the outside ever touched him. He had to engage a woman – my mother – to cook for him, but beyond this he was as near self-supporting as it is possible for a twentieth-century Englishman to be.

Among his few failures was an attempt to grow his own tobacco.

My grandfather died when my father was twenty, leaving him the family business, a small tent and rope factory in Bedfordshire. The factory made many things beside rope and tents: string, matting, canvas, anything that could be made out of hemp. This hemp was grown on a plantation in India, managed in my childhood by one of my father's cousins, a tall, remote man whom we called Uncle Ted. If I had an ideal, Uncle Ted approached it far more than my father. He was lean and burnt out, with colourless eyes like diamonds and enormous feet. I always liked men with big feet, but never married one. Jake's are small, arched, short-toed, inclined to be dainty. When I first met him I thought he was queer, because of the size of his feet and the crumpled little suede shoes he wore on them.

Uncle Ted, my first love, was almost completely silent. Possibly this was because he was stupid, but since he never returned from India after his last journey back in 1936, I don't know. When I was a small child he seemed to me wise. If he is still alive – and there has been no sign of him for twenty-six years – he must be about seventy. In my first term at school I used to carry a photograph of him in my blazer pocket. It was taken against the Indian sun, and screwing up his eyes he looked reasonably boyish. I told the more credulous girls that he was my young man. As I was very fat and plain at the time, even they didn't believe me.

When I grew thinner I fell in love. For two years I loved the son of the local clergyman and he, sporadically, loved me. Although I was only thirteen at the beginning of this romance – he kissed me abruptly on a bus coming back from the cinema in Luton – my parents seemed to approve. I realized later that if they had seen us in bed together they would have thought we were playing sardines. We did not, of course, go to bed together. It didn't occur to us. But we struggled together in the backs of cars, in attics and summer houses and my father's rope yard at night, and in the organ loft. In the term time we wrote to each other, and for the first days of the holidays never sought each other out but waited, with desperate anxiety, to meet by chance in Smith's or Woolworths or outside the bicycle shop, where we would often stand stroking the gleaming handlebars of speedy bicycles.

My friends at school, during this period, were Betty Maclaren, Irene (pronounced Ireen) Douthwaite, Angela Williams and Mary White. Their fathers, like mine, were business men. Their fathers drove twelve-horsepower Standard or Vauxhall cars and wore navy blue suits, trilby hats and mackintoshes. Their mothers all had new permanent waves, made up their faces with vanishing cream and 'natural' face powder, wore fur coats all the year round. Their brothers went to Oundle or Repton and were gods.

When these friends went to stay with each other in the holidays they invented interesting situations between themselves and their friends' brothers. Sometimes a brother would write, 'Give my regards to the fair Angela,' or 'my humblest respects to Miss I. Douthwaite, I hope she is in good health.' Then giggling attacked us like a plague, all day we were wracked with it, spluttering into our handkerchiefs, doubled up over our prayers, not daring to catch each other's eyes for fear of a new bout beginning. I had no brothers, and therefore took it for granted that none of my friends would want to come and stay with me. There had to be a sexual incentive for everything: that was why we went to church and were fairly attentive in scripture, biology and English literature. None of us, at that time, could concentrate on mathematics or geography and we plodded on with Latin only in the faint hope that we might one day be able to understand Ovid. We had not yet encountered medical text-books, which would have provided a sharper spur.

My friends knew, of course, about the clergyman's son. I told them that he was nineteen, since we were only interested in older men, but otherwise I was fairly truthful. 'You wouldn't

like him,' I said airily, keeping my great love for him to myself.
'He doesn't care a bit about films or dance music or anything
like that.'

'Oh, I like clever boys best,' Ireen said, sucking up to me.

'I *dote* on clever boys,' Mary White said. She had an aunt
in London who was going to present her at Court. This same
aunt had already taken her to a play by Noel Coward and a
Cochran revue. Mary White regarded herself as a civilizing
influence and kept telling us that her parents were going to be
divorced. She was not to be trusted.

'Well, you wouldn't like *him*,' I said.

'Why do *you,* then?'

'I don't, all that much. You know how it is. One gets so
dreadfully bored.'

'Oh my goodness,' they sighed, lolling about over their beds
and hitting their open mouths, 'so *bored*, my deah, so too too
too *bored* ...'

'Oh, shut up,' I said, and sulked for the rest of the day,
stalking about with my blazer collar turned up and my lower
lip sagging, to show contempt.

A few days later, when this tiff had been forgotten, Ireen
found me in the library where I was sitting puzzling over a
cross-section of a mighty liner in the *Illustrated London News*.

'I've been looking for you everywhere,' she said. 'I've just
had the most awful news.'

'What news?'

'Well, you know we were going to Spain these hols – '

'Yes. Well?'

'And Roger was going to bring Brian and maybe the Mac-
larens were going to come with Eric and David – '

'Yes. Go *on*.'

'Well! Now it seems we can't go because of this stupid old
war! It just seems we can't go and that's all there is to it!' She
threw a crumpled letter down on the green baize. 'I just got this
letter.'

'What war?' I asked, disbelieving.

'Don't ask me! Some old General's invaded it or something.'

'Invaded what?'

'Spain, you clot. I don't know. Nobody ever tells you a thing in this place. I don't see why we can't go anyway. I mean nobody's going to shoot *us* or anything, are they?'

'Oh no,' I said. 'They wouldn't be allowed to.'

'Well, of course they wouldn't. But Pa says its quite out of the question and we've just got to resign ourselves and go to *Littlehampton*.'

'How awful for you,' I said vaguely. I had never been abroad, and Littlehampton sounded rather distinguished to me.

'Awful? I could die! Of course Roger won't ask Brian *there*. I mean, there's nothing to *do* in Littlehampton. Honestly, I could kill that Franco!'

'Who's he?'

'This old General who's invaded Spain. I mean, it'll probably ruin the rest of my life, not spending these holidays with Brian. I should think we might have got engaged quite easily.'

'I'm sorry,' I said. 'It's jolly bad luck for you.'

'Well, it's all right for you. You've got *Him* to think about.'

'Yes,' I said fondly.

'There'll be no one to talk to in Littlehampton and you know what the boys are like, *common*, and anyway Mummy'll have her eye on me every minute. When I'm with Roger she thinks I'm safe, if only she knew. Oh, I hate that Franco, I hate him, I just hate him!' She plunged her face in her hands and appeared to cry. I was very sorry for her. It seemed brutal to be going home to the intense and uncertain pleasure of the rope-walk and organ loft, and although I had no intention of sharing them with Ireen it did seem to me that she might be quite harmless at the swimming baths or on bicycle rides or in the cinema. It might, in fact, make me seem more independent and casual to the clergyman's son if I took a friend along (that's what I would say: 'I brought my friend along'). Also, although she would discover that he was only seventeen, she would certainly be impressed by his tweed jacket with the leather elbows and the nonchalant way he smoked Gold Flake, without coughing. Then, too, she would help to fill in the unendurable days when he was in one of his moods. We could even go and call at the Vicarage, if there were two of us. We might even be allowed up to his room.

.'Would you like,' I blurted. 'Would you like to come and stay with us for a few days, I mean I know it's not Spain or anything like that, but it might be a bit more fun than Littlehampton, I mean for a bit. Well, you could ask your mother, couldn't you?'

She looked up in the middle of a sob. 'Will *He* be there?'

'Oh yes,' I said recklessly. 'He's always there. He's working very hard, you see. For his Higher.'

'Has He got a friend, do you think?'

'I don't know, I don't actually know his friends. But I mean he must *have* some friends. Well, we could ask.'

'I'd love to come,' she said. 'I really would. I *do* think you're sweet.' She added brightly, and without conviction, 'You must come and stay with us one holiday too. I think you'd get on awfully well with Roger. You're just his type.'

'Thank you,' I said.

'I should think this stupid war or whatever it is will be over jolly soon. Then you could come to Spain.'

'Oh yes,' I said. 'That would be lovely.'

But the war went on and Littlehampton was inescapable for Ireen. She wrote me many anguished letters in which she said that the only thing that prevented her from suicide was the prospect of coming to stay with me 'and meeting *Him*'. I told the clergyman's son, 'My friend, the one who's coming to stay, is terribly unhappy. She was going to Spain, you know. Then she couldn't, because of this war.'

'Gosh,' he groaned, 'Gosh, I wish I could go to Spain.'

'Well, you'll have to wait till after the war, won't you?'

'There won't be any point after the war,' he said. 'You idiot!'

I grew increasingly nervous as the time for Ireen's visit came nearer. I hoped he wouldn't call me an idiot in front of her. He was so unpredictable. My mother, sensing what she felt to be a lack of confidence, arranged for me to have a permanent wave. I refused, and she began to worry about me, dabbing at me all the time to tuck me in or straighten me up or smooth me down. I heard her say to my father, 'She doesn't seem to be like other girls,' and he said, 'Count your blessings, Mame, she's a beauty.' This hardly comforted me. I was not worrying about myself.

Ireen's train arrived in the early evening, so luckily I did not have to make any plans for that day. Tomorrow I would take her round the factory and meet the clergyman's son at the Copper Kettle for what my parents called 'elevenses' and perhaps play tennis in the afternoon. I knew she didn't like reading, and rather doubted whether she would have the patience for mahjong. What would I do with her if it rained? Worrying, I did not notice her as she came up the platform. In any case, I was looking for someone else.

Ireen was wearing what I later heard her describe as a powder blue costume. Her hair was rolled in a perfect sausage at the nape of her neck, and another bobbing over her rather low forehead. She wore high heels, a necklace and lipstick. She was carrying a handbag as well as a suitcase. I thought she looked perfectly frightful. I was horrified. I hardly heard a word she said as we went out of the station and I didn't dare look at the ticket collector, whom I had known all my life. All the way home in the taxi – my father had gone in the car to a meeting of the Cricket Club – I answered her in terrified monosyllables, keeping my bare toes clenched inside my sensible sandals, feeling the sweat of embarrassment behind my knees and in the barely perceptible folds of my breasts. Oh God, I prayed, make her have a bath, make her put on some proper clothes – oh God, *please* don't let her be like this. She had gone to the fair, she said, with a boy from the chemist's and her mother had been simply livid. 'Gosh,' I said dully, hoping we would have a crash in which our corpses would be mutilated beyond recognition. Her lipstick, newly applied, had come off on her front teeth. I felt sick with shame for her.

My mother, after a slight buck of astonishment, took Ireen very well.

'Of course you're a good deal older than this one,' she said, giving me a brisk pat. She frequently called me 'this one', as though I were one of a litter, and always accompanied it with this affectionate cuff which was sometimes quite painful.

'She's not,' I said bleakly. 'She's younger.'

'I'm fourteen and a half,' Ireen said, 'but of course everyone thinks I'm at least eighteen.' She gave me a nasty, tolerant look and added, 'In the holidays.'

'Well, there you are!' my mother exclaimed pointlessly. 'This one will be fifteen in November and look at her!'

They both looked at me and I hated them. I was clean, I was thin, and – a great rush of warmth came over me – I was loved. For all my lack of waves and beads and grubby swansdown puffs and lilies of the valley, I was loved, which was more than they were. I couldn't say this to my mother, but she seemed to sense it because she gave me a quick, conspirator's smile and I almost thought she winked. 'Of course there are those,' she said, slapping my bottom as she passed by, 'who can put up with her ...'

It was not so bad, after that, being left alone with Ireen. She talked incessantly as she unpacked, and I sat on the window sill looking down at the ugly town with its church spire soaring steady and grave above the mess of houses. In one great leap from here I could alight on the spire; then swoop, with a graceful diving motion, through his bedroom window, drifting about his bent head like vapour, pouring myself into his ears and mouth, wreathing myself round him warm, searching, invisible as air ...

'Are you meeting Him tonight?' Ireen asked.

'No. Tomorrow.'

'I simply can't wait. I'm sure he's absolutely gorgeous.'

'We might play mahjong if you like tonight. My father's got a craze for it.'

So after supper, indeed, we played mahjong. My father was very courteous to Ireen, explaining about the four Winds and so on, and he even built her wall for her, which I thought was unnecessary. She had changed into a sort of crepe dress, which I guessed had once belonged to her mother. She giggled a great deal, just as she did at school; but while at school it seemed perfectly natural, I found myself wondering now what she found so funny, and why the simplest word from my father could set her off on this uncontrollable spluttering.

'You must bring Ireen to the works,' my father said. 'That is, if she'd be interested?'

'Oh *yes*!' Ireen said, 'I should adore that!'

'We're coming tomorrow morning anyway,' I said. 'Don't you remember?'

'Show her all your old haunts,' he said, as though I were a ghost.

'But we arranged it already!' I insisted. 'You said to come to the office about ten o'clock. Don't you remember?'

'Did I, dear? Now Ireen, you can't throw away your bamboos in that reckless fashion . . .'

At last we went to bed. Ireen put her hair in curlers and did extraordinary things to her face, slapping it smartly with the back of her hand and covering it with grease. 'You can read my magazines if you like,' she said. 'It says in one of them you must do this *every* night if you don't want a double chin by the time you're twenty. They have terribly serious articles too, you know, about cancer and having the curse,' she giggled briefly, 'and what to do if your husband is unfaithful and all that. Of course Mummy's never told me a thing, but those magazines are most awfully frank, you really should read them.'

'I'm reading *Jane Eyre*,' I said. It sounded priggish, perhaps, but I was in some ways very stupid.

'But that doesn't *tell* you anything! I mean, look here.' She pulled a magazine off her bed and opened it at random. ' "I am fifty-one years old and have recently experienced some pain and difficulty in relations with my husband. I am afraid that this may have a bad effect on our married life, and I have already noticed a slight cooling off on my husband's part. Can you help me before it is too late? Signed Anxious Wife." And the woman says, "This is a condition known as kraurosis, which is a vaginal shrinkage due to hormone withdrawal in middle age. In most cases the use of a special cream will restore normal elasticity. Your doctor will be able to help you if you go to him." Well, I mean, they tell you things like *that*, and it's terribly useful because no one else would, would they? I bet your mother's never even *said* the word vagina to you, has she?' She giggled hopefully and I answered, with complete truth, 'No, she hasn't.' If the woman had a sore throat, I couldn't see what it had to do with her marriage, or why she should write to a magazine about it. 'What else does it tell you?' I asked curiously.

'Well, there's a great long bit about Princess Elizabeth in this one, and a cut-out picture of Clark Gable, and it says what to do about your spots. Oh, oodles of things. You really ought to read them, you know. They'd do you much more good than that old *Jane Eyre*.'

'I'll have a look at them tomorrow,' I said. 'Thanks.'

'They'd help you like anything with *Him*,' she said, bundling into bed and winding her watch, which she then laid carefully on the bedside table. 'I know, because I tried it on Brian last holidays. It works like magic.'

'What does?'

'You know. Keeping them at a distance, being a bit snooty to them. It drives them absolutely *wild*, honestly.'

'Supposing you don't feel snooty?'

'Well, of course you don't, barmy. You just pretend to. I mean, the worst thing of all is running after a boy. It's absolutely *fatal* . . .'

She talked on for what seemed most of the night. I dreamed

I was running after the clergyman's son, running and running with outstretched arms, and when the elastic snakes got in my way I tried to fly over them ... It was very unpleasant and when I woke up I had been crying. Ireen said, 'You're quite different in the holidays. I don't know why.' Miserably, I watched her as she drenched her face in pink powder and clasped on her beads. When we went to the factory I let my father take her round, which he did with great charm, as though she were Royalty. Nobody could see how awful she was. On the way to the Copper Kettle she took my arm and said, 'I do believe you're afraid I'm going to steal him from you. Well, you needn't worry, you know. One thing I am, and that's *loyal*.' As she said this she stopped and rearranged her fringe in front of Sainsbury's window. 'Mary was petrified, you know, that Graham would like me best. Well, I simply froze him off. After all, Mary's my best friend – next to you, of course.'

'I don't think he'd like you to ... freeze him off,' I said. 'He likes people to be nice to him.'

'But of course I'll be *nice* to him! I just mean you needn't *worry*. I mean, he's your boy-friend. I'm just a dear old goose-berry.'

After we had waited for ten minutes in the crowded tea shop, he came lumbering through the door. My heart leapt and I could feel myself growing pale, my knees under the gingham tablecloth began to tremble. 'There he is,' I whispered. 'Where?' 'There, by the door.' 'You mustn't *wave* to him like that! He'll think you want to see him!' 'Well, I do want to see him!' 'Hush, here he comes. I say, isn't he *tall* ...' She moved up on the oak pew, making room for him.

'Hullo,' I said.

'Hullo,' he said.

We smiled at each other and he clapped his hands together, knocked against a woman at the next table, apologized, at last fitted himself into the pew with his back to Ireen.

'This is Ireen,' I said.

He swivelled round, pulling the tablecloth with him. There was demerara sugar all over the place. He slapped about with a rather dirty handkerchief and Ireen said it didn't matter at all. He then said, 'How do you do?' and held out his big hand which grew out of his rather skimpy sleeve like a beautiful cabbage. She shook it delicately. He then sat on his hands, as though to prevent further damage.

'I've heard so much about you,' Ireen said. Her eyelids were fluttering as mine did when I was trying not to cry. I thought perhaps she had hurt herself in the scuffle. 'It's so nice to meet you at last.'

'Well,' he said. But nothing came after. He was staring at her. Her eyelids beat up and down and for some reason she had clenched the tip of her tongue between her teeth and was smiling at the same time. This gave her the look of a complete maniac. At least two whole minutes went by, while I held my breath and wondered what on earth was happening. Was she having a fit? Was this normal? Should I scream or faint or simply carry on with the conversation?

'Are you going to have an ice cream?' I said.

'No. No. I can't stop. I can't stay. I've got to . . .'

'Oh, but you *must*!' Ireen said, and put her hand on his arm, at the same time impossibly moving her body at least six inches towards him. 'You simply *must* stay!'

Now I knew that in daylight, in public places, the clergyman's son was untouchable. To brush against him by accident was enough to send him crashing away, hair tossing, arms flailing, a fearful embodiment of terror and disgust. Therefore when Ireen assaulted him, so to speak, I drew in my breath, knowing what would happen. He leapt up as though shot, took two steps backwards and overturned a hatstand, whirled round and hit a small child over the head with his great uncontrollable hand, bent sideways, grabbed the hatstand, looked desperately at the screaming child, dropped the hatstand, leapt over the pile of fallen coats straight into a waitress with a tray, turned, gasped, gave a hunted cry and was gone. I let out my breath and took a mouthful of ice cream. The café reassembled itself round me with sounds of protest and distress.

'What a pity,' I said. 'He doesn't like you.'

'Doesn't *like* me?'

'You have to be very careful with some boys,' I said. 'You have to know how to deal with them.'

'If you think he ran away like that because he didn't *like* me –' she shouted, outraged.

I licked my spoon, stroking my tongue with it. 'I know he did.'

'Well, that just shows how ignorant you are! That just shows! He was absolutely mad about me! Didn't you see the way he looked at me?'

'Yes,' I said. It was the first time I had ever felt completely grown up – calm, amused, comfortable as my father in his armchair after a good dinner. 'Would you like another ice cream?'

'No, I wouldn't! And I think you're the most awful beast, saying a thing like that! You're just a silly little baby who doesn't know anything, and another thing, you're the most awful hostess I've ever known. You're just green with jealousy, that's your trouble, and I can't be bothered with you and your stupid vicar's son or whatever he is. I'm going home to pack now and I'm jolly well going back to Littlehampton. So good-*bye*!'

I wandered out into the warm morning feeling so happy and smooth and agreeable that even my reflection in Sainsbury's window seemed beautiful. I walked slowly up the street, humming to myself, and when I came to the churchyard my body wheeled to the right without the slightest trouble, and I found myself hopping over the graves, even leap-frogging a tombstone, without a doubt in my mind about where I was going, or why. His bedroom window looked over the churchyard, and this had always seemed to me lugubrious for him; now it seemed proper that he should live so, among the pure and dignified dead. I hop-scotched for a few minutes on the broad paving outside the church door, then sauntered towards the Vicarage. I hardly hesitated before ringing the bell. While I was waiting I leant against the side of the porch and idly chewed a churchyard grass. The door was finally opened by a maid who looked as though she had not been out in the light for a very long time. I asked for the clergyman's son.

'He's not in,' she said.

'Oh.' Should I tell her I'd wait? But no, the gesture had already been made. I had not exactly run after him, but at least I had come this far. 'Tell him . . .' I said, and pondered.

'Yes?' So great was the magic that surrounded me that she seemed eager, even pitifully anxious to know what she should tell him.

'Tell him . . . I called,' I said.

She nodded solemnly. I raced back across the churchyard, through the gate, up the hill, so full of energy that I had to catch railings as I passed, jump gutters, leap for overhanging lilac. 'I love my love with a B because he is BATTY!' I sang. As I burst in through the front door I ran straight into my mother. She steadied me, then not waiting for me to get my breath back she said, 'Ireen is upstairs. She says you were both extremely rude to her and that she wants to go home. I don't know *what* Mrs Douthwaite would think, so I want you to go straight up and tell Ireen you're sorry. Now,' she added, as I hung back. 'This minute.'

We patched it up. I knew Ireen had never intended to go back to Littlehampton, anyway. She hadn't the courage. My parents made a great fuss of her for the remainder of her stay, and she took advantage of this and began to behave as though she were their guest, not mine. This suited me well, for it left me time to myself. The clergyman's son remained in hiding, and for all her conviction that he was dying with love for her, Ireen did not suggest that we tried to find him. It was a hard job, keeping her entertained, even with my parents' help. There was only one cinema in the town, and we saw both programmes. Most of the time she was making her extraordinary faces at the boys in the row behind, so I don't think she would have noticed if we had seen both films twice; but she was so cross when they did not follow us home that she swore she'd gone right off going to the pictures and wouldn't care if she never went again. It was the same story at the tennis club. Only well-brought-up boys played tennis, and she scared them off the courts the moment she appeared.

'Don't you know *any* boys?' she said, conveniently forgetting the clergyman's son. 'I mean, *aren't* there any boys in this place?'

'You met two today,' I said. 'The ones who let us have their court.'

'Oh, *them*! They're children! I think the thing is that I really prefer older men. You know. Men with poise.'

I realized, of course, that she was going to have a hard time making up any stories about her stay with me. Supposing she left without one conquest? She was getting desperate. The bus conductor whistled at her as she got off the bus one day, and that put her in a good temper. But one bus conductor didn't make a summer. Secure, patient in my love for the clergyman's son I didn't see what was happening. I just longed for her to leave, so that I could be free again. My mother said, 'You're keeping a certain person at the Vicarage very far from Ireen, I notice.' My mother could be a bitch at times, in her well-meaning way: or perhaps, like me, she was just stupid. It's often hard to tell the difference, even in oneself.

On the last night of her stay Ireen put on an evening dress, if you please. 'Mummy thought you might dress for dinner,' she said. 'Of course we weren't to know ... Well, anyway, I'd hate her to see I hadn't worn it.' 'My goodness,' my father said. 'This calls for a celebration.' He gave her a glass of elderberry wine – she said she often had wine at home – and during supper I noticed that she was making her faces at him, and that far from being terrified, as any normal person would be, he seemed to be quite interested in them. After supper we played mahjong as usual, but Ireen giggled so much – she had persuaded him to give her some more wine at supper – that it was a hopeless game, and at about half past nine my mother said, 'You're looking peaky, dear. Don't you think she's looking peaky, George? And Ireen has got a long day tomorrow, so I think we should all have an early night.' She tipped her bricks into the box without waiting for argument. 'Come along now. Bedtime for the ladies!'

Ireen scowled. I could see that it was a little undignified, going to bed at half past nine in full evening dress. But no one argued with my mother. We all trooped up the stairs together, my mother bringing up the rear. She kissed us both briefly – she was a scrupulously fair woman in many ways – and told us not to talk too late. I could feel her relief as she shut the door on us and marched off to her own room. Ireen sat down on her bed and began biting her nails. There seemed to be nothing I could say – everything had gone too far – so I undressed and put on my pyjamas and went off to the bathroom to do my teeth without a word of comfort for her.

When I came back she was busy at the dressing table. I hardly glanced at her; just said 'Excuse me' as I reached for my hair brush. When I had finished my hundredth stroke I lay down in bed, dropped my arms like heavy weights outside the covers and shut my eyes. After what seemed like five minutes I opened my eyes again. She was still at the dressing table. I said, 'You're being an awfully long time. Do buck up, I'm dropping.'

She didn't answer, because she was busy doing something to her mouth. I sat up and stared at her. 'What on earth are you putting lipstick on for?'

She capped the lipstick and put it down carefully. Then she swivelled round on the stool. Her face was brand new, she had made up every inch of it. 'If you think I'm going to bed at half past nine,' she said, 'you're crazy.' Her voice shook a little.

'What are you going to do, then?' I asked.

'Go downstairs again, of course.'

'But you can't! Suppose Mummy finds you?'

'If you think I care about your mother,' she said, 'you're crazy.'

'But what are you going to *do*?'

She took a breath, looked at me and swallowed it. Then she got up in her evening dress and went to the light switch, acting just like a mother in a story by Galsworthy. 'Goodnight,' she said sweetly, 'Sleep well.' Then she turned out the light and was gone. I did not hear her go down the stairs. She must have taken her shoes off.

I lay awake for about half an hour, waiting for her to come back. I was frightened about what my parents would say if they found her wandering about the house after bedtime. Anyway, I thought, my father was downstairs. He would deal with her. When I woke up again it was midnight. She had not come back. I thought vaguely of going to look for her, but fell asleep while wondering where to look. The next morning she was neatly tucked up in bed, but had not taken her make-up off. It had streaked all over her face; she looked as though she had been left out in the rain. I spoke to her hesitantly.

'Was it all right ... last night?'

'Was what all right?' She was again the Ireen I knew at school: arrogant, off-hand, not bothering about herself.

'Well, I mean ... did they find you?'

She laughed at me. 'I'll leave you those mags,' she said. 'You ought to read them sometime.'

'Thanks. I will.'

'And good luck with that vicar's son of yours. I suppose you'll be necking with him again now – when I've done gone, I mean.'

My father drove us to the station. Ireen kissed us both good-bye. 'Thanks,' she said, 'for the most gorgeous time.'

'Come again,' my father said. 'We'd love to have you.'

'Thank you,' she said. 'I'll remember that.'

My father and I looked at each other blankly when the train had gone. 'Well, old thing,' he said. 'Back to work.' I followed him out of the station, and the strange thing was that I felt sad. It was almost as though Ireen had stolen the clergyman's son from me after all. I felt deserted, and puzzled, and sad.

10

My father loved me, I know, in his self-sufficient way. For years he regretted that I wasn't a boy, but after Ireen's visit his attitude seemed to change and during the following, the Christmas holidays, he really began to take some sort of tentative pride in me. My mother too stopped pushing and shoving me quite so much, and resigned herself to my straight hair. I began reading the women's magazines, starting with the ones that Ireen had left behind, and learned many useful facts such as that all men are children, all men are emotionally immature, all men dislike hairnets and criticism, all men are unfaithful, must be trusted, need hot breakfasts, want more than they should have and need more than they are given. As I never thought of the clergyman's son as a man, I didn't apply any of this to him. I would not believe, even when he changed so strangely, that he was childish or half-witted – and there, according to Ireen, I made my mistake.

We met as usual on the second day of the holidays. He was staring into the window of the bicycle shop, where all the torches and spanners were wreathed in tinsel. I was wearing an old overcoat of my mother's, since I had grown out of last winter's, and had belted it tightly with a short luggage strap. I had also dabbed my nose with my mother's natural powder and was wearing a suspender belt: but this he couldn't possibly have known. He had grown even taller and his wrists were blue with cold. When I said hullo he whirled round, knocking over two scooters. I propped them up again while he stammered, 'Hullo ... Gosh ... Didn't see you ... I was just ...'

'No. No, I can't. I have to ... Which way are you going?'

'Oh, down the High Street. Are you going down the High Street?'

'No ... Must dash home, do some work ...' He peered at me through the flag of hair that continually fell over his eyes. He combed it through with his fingers and said, 'Gosh. You've changed.'

'Have I?' I should have said no, I haven't, and told the truth.

'Yes. Well ... Good-bye.'

I was sad, but not heart-broken. He had often behaved like this in the past. On my way home I called in at the factory to see my father. He greeted me warmly, and for the first time the clerks stood up when I came in. 'I'm just going to do the tour,' he said – every week he went round seeing every man, woman, and boy, this was his great argument for private enterprise – 'Come along, they'd like to see you.'

So he conducted me round the factory – seeming to forget that I had known it all my life, every dry-smelling, dusty corner of it – and introduced me to the men, most of whom had let me work their looms since my arms were eight inches long, many of whom had saved me from being scalped in the rope-walk or stabbed to death by the great matting needles. I appreciated this, realizing that I had a new status. I bowed gravely to the Mongol boy who wound the rope round huge reels; his top-heavy head nodded like a mandarin and his arms made winding motions all the time he was awake. I sat on a stool in the office, with its water-colours of Kashmir and the Punjab, and examined my grandfather's quill pens, pretending it was the first time. 'I suppose it's not impossible,' my father said, as we drove home for lunch, 'for a women to run a business ...' Then he made a wry face and patted my knee, rejecting the idea.

I didn't see the clergyman's son again until Christmas Day. He and his mother – a silly, insipid woman I thought her – sat in the pew in front of us in church, and all through the service I loved, with a new element of pain, the tender back of his neck, the shoulder-blades in the school suit, the raw, clumsy hands clasped (was he praying?). As we filed out of the church he smiled at me, and in the porch he said, 'Happy Christmas.'

'Happy Christmas.'

'What did you get?'

'Oh ... lots of things. A gramophone. What did you get?'

'I got a gramophone too.' It was a delightful coincidence. We were really pleased. I longed so much to kiss him that I felt weak, almost tearful in spite of my pleasure.

'We might go to the flicks next week,' he said.

'Oh, yes. Yes, that would be lovely.'

'I'll come round on Wednesday.'

'*Yes* ... But oh no, I can't! I can't on Wednesday! I've got to go to this awful old Rotary thing with my father –'

'It doesn't matter.' He had already turned away.

'But it does matter! You see, Mummy hates going, so he said this year he'd take me, and I don't *want* to go either! Can't we go on Tuesday?'

'No, I can't go on Tuesday,' he said. 'It doesn't matter.' And he was off across the churchyard in his navy blue overcoat and new Christmas scarf. Six months before, I would have run after him. Now I stood still among the church-goers, my gloved hands clenched in my pockets, calling out inside myself don't go, don't go, please, I love you so much ...

'You'll ruin the *hang* of that coat,' my mother said, 'if you put your hands in the pockets like that. You must learn that good clothes have to be *worn* well, otherwise you'll always look a little rapscallion.'

So on Wednesday my father took me to the Rotary dinner, where I was given a gilded powder compact engraved with my mother's initials. It was intensely boring, but they all made a great fuss of me and I began to think that perhaps it was better to be bored and admired than interested and miserable. I tried flapping my eyelashes and was amazed when old men I had known all my life went pink, and giggled, and even offered me cigarettes. 'She behaved beautifully,' my father told my mother, who was waiting up with Ovaltine. 'A perfect lady. It's something, you know, to have a daughter you can be proud of.'

'Handsome is as handsome does,' my mother said. 'You shouldn't say such things in front of the child, George. She'll get swollen-headed.'

I did, a little. The next week my mother took me to London for the day and bought me an evening dress at Debenhams, yellow net with a yellow taffeta underskirt and a clutch of hard yellow rosebuds on the bodice. I was stupid enough to long for the clergyman's son to see me in it, though if he had, he would have run a mile. On Saturday night my father took me to the Masonic Ball.

This, the peak of the town's New Year celebrations, was held in the largest hotel, one of remarkable dinginess and squalor. That night, with streamers and balloons, changing spotlights, and a band dressed in satin Cossack shirts, it was transformed. I danced with my father, who did a surprisingly elegant slow foxtrot, and with the bank manager and the manager of Boots and a reporter who was not a Mason but had to write about the Ball for the local paper. I was sipping fruit cup, a little out of breath, when Mr. Simpkin asked me for the pleasure.

He was a small, square man, Mr Simpkin, with too much face for the size of his features : his little sparking eyes and snub nose and small, fat mouth sat very close together in a great expanse of cheek. As though to fill up his face he wore a thin, spiky moustache, gingerish. His hair, thinning, was fixed across the top of his head in separate strands. He held me quite differently from the others, clasping my hand close and gently pressing his hard, round stomach against me. He was a beautiful dancer, and his patent leather feet seemed to draw mine after them like magnets.

'Enjoying yourself?' he asked.

'Oh, yes. Yes, I am.'

'I'm an old friend of your father's, y'know. I saw you at the

Rotary do last week. I suppose they all tell you you look like Hedy Lamarr?'

'No. No, no one does.' Curious, I flapped my eyelashes a little. 'Why? Do I?'

'You do indeed.' He held me a little closer. 'How old are you, anyway?'

'Sixteen,' I lied.

'Still at school, I suppose?' He murmured these questions, hardly opening his mouth.

'Yes. But I'm leaving soon. I've had enough of school.' This was true, but I had never even thought it before. The music stopped and we clapped, but he did not lead me away.

'Let's have the next,' he said, twinkling. 'Your father knows you're quite safe with me.'

It seemed that Mr Simpkin was the manager of a near-by paper works.

'You must come along sometime,' he said. 'I'll show you around. There's a lot to interest a bright girl like you. How about it, one afternoon? Then we could have a spot of ... tea, and I'll deliver you back safe and sound.'

'It'd be simply lovely.'

'That's a date, then. Keep it to ourselves, shall we? You'd better give me a ring.'

It was almost an assignation. He must have felt my delight because he cooled off a little, and after that dance took me to meet his wife. She was sitting with the other wives on a sofa in a kind of crypt just off the ballroom. Mr Simpkin introduced me as 'George's little girl – you remember?' and she talked to me kindly. All I saw of her was a mottled turkey neck hung with pearls and rough, working hands which she had tried to cover with talcum powder.

After this, the holidays settled down, more boring, more empty than they had ever been before. I waited for the clergyman's son to call, but he didn't come. I loved him more, if anything, but my love now grew anxious, sharp, even resentful. I even told myself that I hated him, which was an elaboration of love that I couldn't understand and which filled me with misery. Twice I met him in the town, but the first time he stumbled into the fishmonger's and the second time he ran as though all the hounds of hell were after him across the church-yard. Still I couldn't believe that he didn't want to see me. I defied the women's magazines and rang him up, but his mother answered and said that he was working and she was very, very reluctant to disturb him since everything depended on his passing the Higher Certificate since without the Higher Certificate he would be unable to go to Oxford, which would be a great deprivation since his father was quite set on him going to St John's which was his father's old college and had quite a remarkably pretty garden, I must go and see it if ever I went to Oxford, but in the meanwhile ... So I wrote him smudged letters, and tore them up. My mother said I had had too much excitement, and for some reason became angry with me. The days at home were stiff and hostile and I spent hours in my hot bedroom, wishing I could die.

Two days before the end of the holidays my mother went to a meeting of the Townswomen's Guild, leaving me alone in the house. I walked from room to room looking for something to do. My body ached. I wanted to run, leap, stretch, exhaust myself, but somehow I was too tired. I made faces at myself in the hall mirror. Suddenly, without any warning, the afternoon became intolerable. It was something I couldn't live through, an impossibility. Wondering at myself, but with a curious sense of obedience, I telephoned Mr Simpkin at the paper works.

'I must see you,' I said. 'Immediately.'

'Well, well. My goodness. And how are you, my dear?'

'I want to see you straightaway.'

'Is something ... the matter?'

'Shall I come to the works?'

'No, no. No, don't do that.' There was a short pause. 'You're at home, I take it?'

'Yes, but they're all out.'

'Well ... I don't think I should come to the house.'

'All right,' I said. 'I'll meet you at the end of the drive. We can go up Sam's lane.'

Sam's lane was the nearest childhood walk. I don't think I imagined Mr Simpkin and me trudging down it for the good of our health. I don't think I imagined anything. Sam's lane was the obvious place to go, since it was out of the town, which was ugly, and not right in the country, which was too far. I went upstairs and put on a jersey dress, cut on the bias, which I thought suited me, and my school mackintosh. Something told me that this would be more appropriate than my new, well-hanging overcoat. Then, giving Mr Simpkin exactly time to tell his staff that he was going out for a while, to put on his coat and hat and drive from the paper works, I walked down to the gate.

Not, as my mother thought afterwards, to my doom – Mr Simpkin merely kissed me, his moustache grazing my gums like a toothbrush, and fumbled a little with the unyielding navy gaberdine. Obviously he thought that this was what I wanted, and looking back on it I could not blame him if he had raped me. But rape, thank God, is not for the Mr Simpkinses of this world. They are level-headed men, sane men, men who know what's what. A little flirtation with a willing partner, even if it's a schoolgirl who telephones you at three in the afternoon, is just as far as a reasonable man like Mr Simpkin cares to go on his home ground. On a business trip, of course, it's different – well, a man's got to have a bit of sport, a good story to take back to the boys, what the wife doesn't see the wife doesn't grieve over and there's nothing nasty about it, you understand, nothing what you might call *sexual*. Much of this, in that ten minutes up Sam's lane, I began to understand.

'I think you'd better take me home now,' I said.

'Oh, come on, duckie.' He was panting heavily and his moustache was wet. 'Give me another kiss.'

'If you don't take me home, I shall walk,' I said.

'What's the matter? You said you wanted to see me!'

'Well. I've seen you. Please will you take me home?'

So he did, as far as the bottom of the drive. He looked puzzled.

For the rest of the day I lay on my bed, or more accurately rolled and tossed and curled up like a spring on my bed, in a state of horror. My mother cajoled, shouted, even slapped me at one point, but I was speechless. Whenever she went out of the room I called desperately on the clergyman's son to save me, but when she came back again I simply howled and hiccuped, feeling as though there were a great gale in me which I could not contain, a storm so violent that I need not even try to control it. I must be saved, I thought, I must be saved. From what? I didn't know, but later I began to know. The nervous boy, whom I loved, was good. Mr Simpkin was evil. I wanted to be delivered from evil by love, and never to touch it again for the rest of my life. Not for me the sofa at the Masonic Ball, the dirty joke, the quick bash; not for me spite, deceit, disgust. Save me, I implored the clergyman's son, please save me. I didn't know, of course, that this conception of salvation was completely idiotic, and that no man, woman or child can be another's saviour. I did not even know this twenty-six years later, when I talked to Bob Conway in my own delightful sitting-room and recognized once more the brutality that for half a life time I had called Mr Simpkin.

Around supper time my mother called the doctor in. He said it was my age, and gave me a couple of pink pills. Before I went to sleep I told her all about it. She was exceedingly shocked and said we must keep it from my father. She didn't know I even knew about such things, she protested; she didn't know I had a side like that to my character at all. Whatever came over me, she asked, whatever possessed me? I sobbed into my slimy pillow that I didn't know. I never saw Mr Simpkin again. Possibly he left the neighbourhood. Eighteen months later, in the clergyman's church, I was married to the reporter I had met at the Masonic Ball. The clergyman's son passed his

Higher Certificate and went up to Oxford, where he became a homosexual. I had a great affection for him, for many years.

II

'What is Jake's ... *background*?' the doctor asked.

'Background?'

'Is his background the same as yours or is there a ... conflict there?'

'Why do you always ask me about Jake? I come here and all you ask me is about Jake. I've only known the man for thirteen years, he's not my father, my brother, he's not even my Uncle Ted. Perhaps it's Jake you should be seeing. Not me.'

I looked at him quickly, to catch him out. He was staring rather drearily at some point in the air between us: his eyes saw so far, no farther. I thought he held his sight on a leash, pulling it in or extending it at will. I wanted him to see me, but didn't know how to attract his attention. 'What has Jake to do with me?' I asked, realizing too late that the question sounded biblical and absurd.

His sight retired, tortoise-like, into his head. He could now see no farther than the inkstand and gold-embossed leather blotter in front of him.

'I don't want to talk about Jake,' I explained. 'I want to talk about myself.'

'Carry on.' He made a vague, conducting gesture. 'Please. Carry on.'

I sat for a long time, unable to think of anything. At last I said, 'I'm much better, you know. By the time Jake comes back I shall be ... quite better.'

'You find the tablets a help?'

'Yes. A great help.'

'Good, good. Don't get in the habit of taking them.'

'But you told me to take two a day.'

'Yes, of course. But don't get in the habit.'

I tried again. 'Don't you think I seem better?'

'Of course. Every day and in every way ...' Then he became solemn. 'However, you must realize that at the moment we are simply putting stepping stones, shall I say, over a raging torrent. Our task is to divert that torrent. To divert it, as it were, to some other area where it is badly needed. To do that, we must find its source. That can't be done in three or four weeks, you know. We must trace the course of the torrent.' He raised his hands, palms together, and snaked them through imaginary valleys. 'We must trace the course carefully until one day, hidden under some insignificant rock, we shall come upon a small spring and then, *then*, we can talk about getting better.'

I thought about this for a few moments. Then I asked, 'What torrent?'

'We might call it your will to self-destruction.'

'And we have to divert that?'

'We have to turn it into creative channels, yes.'

'I don't honestly know what you're talking about. I mean ...' I frowned, trying to think of a kinder way of putting it, 'I mean, I don't *have* any will to self-destruction.'

'Not consciously, of course. But the pain, the danger you experience in childbirth, for instance, isn't that ...?'

'Oh, really!' I said. 'It's absurd!'

He nodded, smiling, and wrote in his book.

'You can't say it's destructive to have children. Not if you want them. Not if you can keep them.'

'But there was a time when you couldn't keep them?'

'We went into that last time,' I said. 'I could always keep them.'

'But at the cost of at least two marriages.'

'Let's talk about the torrent,' I said. 'It really makes more sense.'

He bowed his head, and for a moment I felt sorry for him. Poor man, the butt of everyone's anger, I should be nicer to him. 'Jake's parents,' I said, 'were quite different from mine.'

'They're dead?'

'His mother is. She died when he was quite young, he doesn't remember her, he doesn't even know what she was like. In the photographs she looks like one of those woman novelists in the '20's, with shirt-waists and those great jackets with slits up the back, like men's. He was looked after by housekeepers, women who didn't really care. There wasn't a loving one among them. I suppose that's why he loved his father so much. I mean, he still loves him. His father treats him like a child, you know, he nags him and baits him, he keeps all the bad notices of Jake's pictures, never the good ones. But it doesn't make any difference. They're the same person. If you want to know what Jake will be like in another thirty years ... there he is. He's more or less retired now, but he used to write crime stories – he wrote hundreds, they were very successful, he made a lot of money. He called himself Max English. Perhaps you read them?'

'No. No. I'm not much of a one for crime.'

'He's selfish, and mean, but ... I'm very fond of him, too. He was away a lot when Jake was a child. Jake was terribly lonely. Lonely and sad at home, and at school. He was at school from the time he was six, and he hated it.'

'Did he go into the army?'

'Well, he did for about eight weeks. Before the war, when he left Oxford, he wanted to be an actor, then he went into advertising for a bit, then he was called up. But there was something wrong with his bladder, so they circumcised him, and when that didn't do any good they let him out.'

'You mean he was discharged?'

'Yes. But the bladder thing got better anyway. He says that was the unhappiest time of his life, but afterwards, when he'd left the army, he enjoyed the war. He worked in the Ministry of Information – I don't quite know what he *did* – but goodness, those were the days.'

'I don't follow you ...'

'For Jake, those were the days. The shelters, the blackout,

everybody not being downhearted. The war did everything for him. It did his feeling for him. I mean, nobody expected anything of *him*, do you see? The whole world was serious and tragic and full of gloom, so people like Jake were let off. It wasn't necessary for Jake to think or feel during the war, or take anything seriously, or care. He didn't have to make up his mind about anything and he was *approved* of. When he talks about the war now it's just like somebody talking about their childhood. You know? It was always summer and always strawberries for tea, there was always someone who loved you for what you were, not for what you ought to be.'

'But of course that's not true.'

'No.'

He looked up at me, smiling. 'Go on. When you first met him, what was he doing?'

'He'd just begun to work in films, but he was only doing re-writes, nothing very much, he didn't even know whether he'd be able to go on. The first time I met him, he came to tea.' I hesitated, but he seemed fairly interested, so I went on. 'Jake was a friend of Giles's and he came down from London, it was a Sunday. We lived in a sort of barn – I told you, I think, that's where we're building the tower – someone had begun to convert it before the war, then when the war came they just left it and we rented it for practically nothing. It was a very sensible place for us really. It was huge, there was nothing inside except a big platform, like a gallery. But it had light and water and drains, because they'd already put them in. Giles collected a lot of hardboard from somewhere – he was very practical, for a violinist – and made dozens of partitions, like loose boxes, he called them areas. So we had these areas for everything, even one for him to play the violin in, but since the walls were only about six feet high the children used to climb over them, though Giles kept telling them he'd left perfectly good pathways. After a bit they got very shaky and some of them fell down, but by that time I think Giles knew it was all over so he didn't bother to fix them up again. They were just left propped about. I was always falling over them with trays ... Anyway, Jake came to tea. I was pregnant, about seven months pregnant, and I was wearing the most dreadful smock, and boots because it was so cold. It must have been chaos. It's funny, I can't remember. I can remember it happening, but not what I thought or felt or what we talked about, except that Dinah sat on Jake's knee. She was nearly four. He always liked Dinah best because her father was dead, also because she was very pretty. He told me afterwards that he fell in love with me then, that afternoon, that he wanted to make love to me. I don't know if it's true. I think he wanted to join us, that's all. I think he wanted ... to belong to us.'

'Yes,' he said. 'Yes.'

'So he married me.'

'Yes.'

'We were very happy.'

'I'm sure you were.'

'He enjoyed everything – things that I'd got so used to, I didn't notice them any more. He used to help put them to bed – I mean, they weren't his, after all – and tell them great stories and play with them. He worked hard, perhaps in a way he worked harder than he does now, but because it was for a different reason it was easier. I find all this hard to explain. Christmas, for instance. When he was a child he hated it, he was all alone, they used to have dinner in the evening and make him wear a dinner jacket and then when the port came he was sent to bed. The first Christmas he knew us he hacked down an enormous tree, much too big, and they all carried it in and he decorated it, he made an angel for the top. Then on Christmas Day he did a play with them but they all laughed so much that ... I'm sorry. I'm sorry.'

'That's all right. Don't worry.'

'Now he sends his secretary to Hamleys and everything comes wrapped, and except for the youngest ones they're all bored and hating it because he does nothing but tell them how expensive it is and how meaningless. And anyway there's nothing to give. That Christmas I gave him a snow-storm, a glass ball.'

He waited for a moment. 'When did his success begin? Some time ago, I take it?'

'He wrote a film about ... Philpot. It was about a girl who went around breaking up people's marriages, but always by mistake, comically. It started with all the ushers in the Divorce Court saying hullo to her in the morning, because they knew her so well. It was sexy and it made people laugh. That was the beginning. It was about eight years ago.'

'And life changed.'

'Not all at once. Of course it didn't. But we bought a lot of things – furniture, machines, cars. We got help. I don't know why it's called help.'

'You mean servants?'

'We don't call them servants.'

'It must have been a relief to you.'

'At first it was. The idea of it was. I imagined I'd have more time for Jake. But we all began to live alone, that's what really happened. We got men in to paint the rooms, and we didn't have to wash up any more, the children didn't come and grate cheese or make biscuits, in the evening they watched television, but not with us, and in the afternoons they went out for walks with the help. We drove about alone in our cars and we went away for holidays without Jake, because he was working. He took an office and ...'

'And what?'

'I don't know. We've managed it badly, I suppose. There's nothing left.'

He sighed, as though he thought the story had been a sad one. Then he asked abruptly, 'Do you like Jake?'

'Like him?'

'Apart from everything else you feel about him, all your conflicting emotions ... Do you like him?'

'No,' I said. 'Not very much.'

'That's my impression. Why don't you like him?'

I tried to think. One by one I turned over the possible reasons for disliking Jake: he is a coward, a cheat, he is mean, vain, cruel, he is slovenly, he is sly. 'I . . . I don't know,' I said.

'But you love him?'

'Yes. Yes, I love him.'

'You want your marriage to survive?'

'Yes.'

'Do you think that in order for your marriage to survive there should be some . . . change?'

'Yes.'

'Do you think Jake is liable to change?'

'No.'

I felt that I had at last given him a correct answer. He folded his file, screwed up his pen, with the air of a man whose backward pupil is beginning, after long weeks of patience and work, to make a little progress. 'Think about what you have just said. Just chew it over a little during the next couple of weeks. Will you do that?'

'Couple of weeks?'

'I shan't be seeing you again for a fortnight. Surely I told you?'

'No – '

'Oh, really – I'm so tremendously sorry. I quite thought I'd told you last time. We're off to Gstadt on Friday for a spot of ski-ing.' He grinned bashfully. 'It's my great passion, I'm afraid.'

'But . . .' I couldn't believe it. Leaving me? Leaving me now? 'But what about . . . ?'

'Keep on with the pills, if you need them. Oh, and cut down on liquids as much as you can. We'll make an appointment, shall we, for the . . . 19th? Would the 19th suit you?'

'I can't manage the 19th. I know I can't.'

'Then why don't you give me a ring in, say, three weeks' time? See how you get on.' He beamed at me, persuasive, bland as a salesman leaving a free sample. No obligation, madam, it's entirely up to you.

'Jake will be back by then. I don't think I shall be able to manage it.'

'Oh, come now ...'

'No,' I said. 'I don't think I shall be able to manage it.'

'But it would be such a pity if you gave up ...'

'If *I* gave up? What do your patients do while you're away? Commit suicide, murder their wives, or do they just sit and cry and take pills and think about what they told you last time? Supposing I take it into my head to get pregnant again? That's my disease, isn't it? Wouldn't it be a great deal simpler just to ... sterilize me, or whatever it is they do, then you could go off to your ski-ing without a care in the world? If I'm sane enough to be left alone with my *thoughts* for two weeks then I'm too sane to need these futile, boring conversations – because my God, they bore me – at six guineas a time. I thought I was meant to ...' I shut my mouth, clenching it tight. The wailing stopped. The room was peaceful. I said carefully, 'It doesn't matter what I thought. I was wrong. I'll go now.'

He sighed again, more deeply, and examined his pen with such close scrutiny that he might have been reading a thermometer. Then he looked up. 'Tell me,' he said, 'how's Dinah? She had 'flu, I think, last time you came.'

'She's better. She's ... taken to Trotsky.'

'Indeed? Why?'

'Somebody told her that he believed in the liberty of the individual.'

'It's a pleasant thought,' he said wistfully. He did not get up when I left. I heard later that he had broken a leg ski-ing. I thought then, blaming him, that if he hadn't gone we might both have remained undamaged.

12

Jake arrived back from North Africa early on Saturday morning, and the children were all home from school. Most of them were in the front bedrooms, watching for him; when they saw his car draw up they cateracted down the stairs, swarming over him as he came through the front door, disregarding the clipped cries of the nurse. The violinist's children flung themselves bodily, but his own stood holding him like a maypole. Dinah was not there. I called for her, but she didn't answer. I could only see the top of Jake's head as I came down slowly, smiling, step by step. He seemed to be being eaten.

'Hullo ... Hullo ... Hullo, there ... How's my baby?' (This to the youngest, held up by the nurse.) 'Go on, then, get the things out of the car ... Where's Mum? ... Go on, unload the car, can't you? ... Where's Dinah? Where's Mum? ... No, I haven't brought you anything, you haven't been good enough ... Is Mum still in bed? Where's Mum?'

'Here,' I said, and hurried the rest of the way. His coat was damp, his face darkly sunburned. The children fell back a little and we embraced self-consciously.

'It's lovely to have you back,' I said.

'Lovely to be back.'

'You do look well.'

'I'm bloody tired actually.'

'Would you like some ... coffee or something?'

'No thanks. I need a drink.'

'Well ... come in.'

The older children staggered in with the suitcases, grasping the handles in both hands, straining backwards against the weight, making a great fuss. They dropped them about the room and the younger children undid them, rummaging about among dirty shirts to find packages. Jake helped them energetically, after one of them had poured him a large brandy and another had put too much soda in it.

'Where is Dinah, anyway?'

'Oh, she's still in bed.'

'She hasn't been well,' I said quickly.

'Oh ... here ...'

I put on a vaguely Moorish dressing-gown, pure rayon and covered with the signs of the Zodiac; they all admired it and Jake said uneasily, 'It's meant to bring you luck. I got one for Dinah too.'

'I'm sure she'll love it.'

'There's nothing to buy, really. You know, just a lot of junk.'

'It's lovely. Really it is.'

'Well. Anyway ...'

'I got a green star ... I got top in Friday Paper ... Two of the goldfish died and a cat ... Did you see any lions? ... I got a green star for spelling and I got ... Well, *I* got top in Friday Paper ... What were the elephants like, did you see any lions? ... We went to the circus, we went to the pictures three times ... That's where I fell down ... Did you see any camels, then? ... *and* I got a green star for sums ... I didn't have a plaster, I had a bandage ... So can we have some more goldfish, and can we have a *dog* ... Would you like to see my Scripture book? Was it a Jet? Did you see any hyenas? Can we have *tropical* fish? ... That's Moses, that's David, that's Joseph in prison ...'

The welcome slowly burned itself out. At last they grew bored and drifted away, some guiltily, saying they would soon be back, some with relief. Jake reached for my hand.

'Well?' he asked. 'How are you?'

'I'm ... fine.'

He patted his knee. 'Come and tell me all about it. Give me a drink first.'

I gave him a drink and knelt, leaning against his leg.

'I wish you'd been there,' he said. 'We had a wonderful

time. Of course Hurst and Dante hated each other on sight ...'
I listened, content. Jake was a great gossip, he enjoyed specula-
tion and intrigue and seldom disliked anyone. The few people
he did dislike were overbearingly sincere, intensely serious and
tinged with failure: these he dismissed as bores, and they did
not enter his world.

I listened, and waited.

'What about the rest of the unit? Are they back?'

'Beth and John came back with me.' He yawned one of his
enormous yawns, his eyes watering. 'Doug's coming tomorrow,
we're starting at Elstree on Wednesday.'

'And what about Dante, whatever she's called?'

'Oh, we got rid of her at the beginning of the week. She
went off somewhere to buy a bit of Balmain. Anyway ... what
about you?'

'I'm fine. Really.'

'Have you been going to that chap, that doctor?'

'Yes. Yes, I have.'

'Oh well, then ...' He shook his head to clear his eyes. 'God,
I'm tired. I suppose it's Saturday morning ...'

'Yes.'

I could see Saturday morning creeping over him. He looked
round the room. Some children were shooting each other out
in the cold garden. A radio, a gramophone and a clarinet were
being played in various parts of the house. The smell of roasting
joint seeped under the door. His face seemed to gather sadness
and he repeated heavily, 'Oh well, then ...' and gave a great
sigh. 'Oh well, I suppose ...'

'I'm sorry,' I said.

'Sorry?'

I held his knees tightly, unable to explain. The party's over.
Poor Jake, poor Jake. There ought to be champagne and calling
people up, flowers and friends and a hotel suite where you ring
for the ice ... But no. There is carving the joint and quarrelling
about the cauliflower. Poor, poor Jake.

He asked affectionately, 'What's the matter with you?'

'Nothing.' Still easily moved, uncontrollable and easy, my eyes had filled with tears. 'Nothing. Really.'

He withdrew, nervous. 'There's nothing to cry about.'

'I'm not crying.'

'Is that ... doc doing you any good?'

'He says I think I'm a tea cosy.'

He laughed, but only for a moment. I heard him thinking, weeping wife, kids, bills, joint, Saturday, nothing's changed. It did not occur to me that these were my thoughts, or that his could be more complex. I felt that I could not comfort him alone, and that I must appear to understand his feelings without having them explained to me. I blew my nose and said, 'Why not ask them round?'

'Ask who round?'

'I don't know – John, Beth Conway, even Dante if you know where she is.'

'You mean tonight?'

'Then I could hear all about it. Properly.'

'You mean this evening?'

'Yes. Why not?'

'But ... you don't want them round here *tonight*?'

'Yes, I do. I do. Really.' Why wouldn't he believe me? I was telling the truth. 'Ring them up. Come on, they're probably feeling just as gloomy as you are. You know you want to.'

He looked extremely puzzled: bewilderment and hope, Cinderella sent back to the ball, Jake raised from the dead.

'Oh, no,' he said. 'No. It'd bore you ...'

'If you won't, I will. Where's Hurst staying?'

'At the Connaught. But he'll probably be asleep.'

Hurst was not asleep. He was very drunk. He would come, he said, he would come on the dot, he couldn't wait, my darling, my sweet, oh God the laughs they'd had ...

'Now you ring Beth Conway,' I said.

'No. You ring her. You're so good at it.'

Beth Conway said she would have to ask her husband. There was a long wait. Finally she came back and said in a small voice, 'Yes, Bob says that would be absolutely marvellous. What a splendid idea. Will it be sort of ... dressy, do you think?'

'No, not a bit.' I put my hand over the mouthpiece and said, 'She wants to know if it'll be *dressy*.' He said, on the fringe of a yawn, 'Give her my love.'

'Jake sends you his love.'

'Oh. Thank you. We look forward to meeting you, awfully.'

'Yes,' I said. 'It does seem silly we've never met.'

I went over to Jake and kissed him. He still seemed a little stunned. 'There you are. You can do the rest.'

He grabbed my wrist and pulled me round to face him. 'Have you been having an affair with that doctor or something?'

'How did you guess?'

'Something's happened. You look about eighteen. You look cunning.'

'It's the pills,' I said. 'He gave me pills. They're very rejuvenating.'

'What are you hiding? There's something. What is it?'

'Nothing.'

'You've got some plan, I can tell that. Haven't you got some plan?'

'Of course not.' But as I said it I knew. I might have a plan. How stupid of me not to think of it before. Hated doctor, darling Jake – naturally I have a plan.

13

'Professional men,' Bob Conway said, 'are all alike – doctors, lawyers, parsons, bloody parasites the lot of them. I call myself a tradesman because that's the only thing I've any respect for – a man's trade. Take these head-shrinkers now, you can't call that decent work, man's work, no, not in my honest opinion.

In my honest opinion the whole bunch of them are a lot of frauds. About the only thing these leeches can cure is a case of clap. How about measles, how about mumps – our kid had mumps while Beth was away, so I *know*, I can tell you. How about the common cold, how about a cure for that ? '

He was about fifty, squat, fat, with a throttling bow tie and small, twinkling eyes. His eyes twinkled as though hung in his head to frighten the birds away. He reminded me of someone, but I couldn't think who. I moved round him a little and caught sight of Dinah pinned into a corner by John Hurst. She signalled 'Help!' over his shoulder and turned it neatly into a radiant smile.

'Excuse me . . .' I said, 'but I must . . .'

'We all know what we want,' Bob Conway said, 'and what the hell's the good of wondering why we want it ? Well, I know what I want, and the more of it the better ! ' He nudged me with his empty glass.

'Jake . . .' By stepping back and plunging my arm between two unknown and startled guests, I managed to catch him. 'Mr Conway needs a drink. Can you . . . ? '

I edged over to Dinah. Hurst was clutching the high bookshelf with both hands and had her penned between them. I ducked under one of his arms and rose up next to Dinah. He was incapable, it seemed, of moving and for a few moments, until he fell on me, Dinah and I jostled each other like people in a small lift.

'Darling Mrs Jake!' he said. 'Darling! What about this steaming girl of yours ? Isn't she a beauty ? Isn't she marvellous ? ' At this he fell, enveloping me. Dinah blushed and giggled. 'I've been telling her she should go on the movies. No, honestly. She'd make a fortune. Darling Mrs Jake, where's that old fox of yours been hiding you, you should have been *there* !'

'I wish I – '

'We could have had a marvellous time! You simply abandoned us to that ghastly Dante, you know that.'

'Well,' I said, flicking an eyelid at Dinah, 'there was Beth.'

He lowered his voice to a roar. 'Tiny bit boring, between you and me. Strict secrets, of course. English Rose stuff. Death-ville, as far as I'm concerned. Anyway, she's got the most ghastly breath, haven't you noticed?'

'I haven't ... been very close.'

'Well, believe me she has. Darling! My angel!' He had been clasped from the rear by a thin, faceless girl wearing black leather. She towed him away. Dinah said, 'Gosh, thanks. I thought I was done for.'

'I rather like him.'

'Well, he's certainly marvellous for his age. I say, Dad's very *with* it tonight, isn't he? I didn't know Beth Conway had red hair, I thought it was sort of blonde. She's jolly pretty, I must say, what an awful thing to say about her breath.'

'Do you want to meet someone? There's a cameraman called Ned.'

'I met him, he's a queer coot. I think I'll go to bed if you don't mind. Dad won't notice, will he?'

'I shouldn't think so. Will you look and see if they're all all right?'

'Okay. Good night, then.'

The curious exhilaration of the day was going; I could feel it leaving me empty, lonely, uncertain again. I wanted to touch Jake, to be quiet. Everyone in the room was frolicking in love, splashing each other with love, falling about in it, drinking it, pretending to drown in love. Jake and a tall, spectacled Ameri-can were wreathed together like schoolgirls. Beth Conway was being hugged by Hurst, in spite of her breath. The cameraman was curled up on the continuity girl's lap, nuzzling into her mohair breast. I drank a glassful of champagne that someone had left on the bookcase. It was immediately filled again by Conway who said, 'I'm hanging on to this bottle, it's the easiest way.'

'Oh,' I said. 'Good.' Jack was mobile at parties, relentlessly leaving people in the middle of a sentence, always planning his next move. I seemed to go from trap to trap. I finished the champagne, hoping it would quell a rising despair.

'Somebody told me that gorgeous little blonde is one of your daughters,' Bob Conway said. 'You haven't sent her to bed, have you?'

'She's ... she's gone to bed, yes.'

'How old is she?'

'Sixteen. Well ... nearly seventeen.'

'I suppose everyone tells you you look like sisters?'

'Yes,' I said. 'Nearly everyone.'

'But she's not the oldest, is she?'

'No, she's not the oldest.'

'How old is the youngest, then?'

'Three.' I made a tremendous effort, wrenching my eyes round to look at him. 'How old is yours?'

'Oh, she's two and a half. Prettiest little thing you've ever seen, just like her Mum. We miss Beth, I can tell you, when she has to go away like this.'

'I'm sure you do. I ... miss Jake, too.'

'Well, it gives us the chance for a little ring-a-ding-ding – eh? Next time they go off, I'll give you a tootle. You might like to see round the works.'

I stared at him, unbelieving. 'What works?'

'I run up Hi-Fi, you know, tape recorders, sound equipment, special stuff. It might interest an intelligent woman like yourself.'

I felt myself swaying slightly, unable to balance on my heels.

'I'm not at all intelligent,' I said. 'Not at all.'

'Don't give me that. I know an intelligent woman when I see one.'

'I learnt two things at school,' I said. 'Just two. Shall I tell you what they were?'

'Now don't shock me.'

'Si-Sing,' I began carefully, 'Si-sing est un bon Chinois, ronde comme une pomme et jaune comme un ... motte du beurre.'

'That's French.'

'Right. And the other thing, a corm is the swollen underground stem of an erect shoot. That's all I learned.'

'Well, you seem to have made pretty good use of that last piece of knowledge, ha, ha. Very good use indeed. You must tell Beth that, she's got the smuttiest mind of any girl I know, that's why I married her.' He shook with grim laughter and clutched my arm. I stepped back so wildly that I knocked against a picture on the wall; a screw ripped out and the picture fell to the ground like someone dying. Bob Conway propped it against the wall, consoling it.

'I've been meaning to take that picture down for years,' I said. 'For nine years. Isn't that extraordinary? You know, you remind me of someone, and I can't think who it is. I just can't think. Perhaps Jake would know. Let's go and ask him.'

'I must find Beth and tell her ...' He raised himself on tiptoe, swaying from left to right with his chin high while the remains of the champagne tipped and swilled in the bottom of his glass. 'Where is she? Where *is* Beth?'

'She's over on the sofa,' I said. 'Talking to Jake.'

He looked at me, momentarily sharp, as a man looks at a safe he means to burgle later. My memory struggled. 'Eyes in the back of your head?' he asked.

I smiled, obscurely frightened, and allowed him to grasp my upper arm, steering me in front of him along the length of the room. His grip was too tight, his hand wrapped round my arm like a register of blood pressure. Beth was sitting decorously on the sofa. She was looking down at Jake, who sprawled on the floor holding the neck of a champagne bottle between his straddled knees; but at the moment when I broke through, shielding Conway, she raised her head. With his free hand, Conway signalled to her; she waved back, moving only her fingers, and her face, which had been shadowed and solemn, seemed to blaze with relief. Conway let go of my arm and I sat down by Jake. 'Beth's dying to ask your advice,' he said, stroking the back of my neck. 'I've told her you know all about children.'

'What *she* needs,' Conway said, 'is another half dozen, and quick. Knock some of these fancy ideas out of her head.' He squeezed her as he said it, and sounded tender.

'Oh, really, Bob! You're so old-fashioned. Anyway, Jake's got a marvellous idea for a new movie.' She gazed at me damply. Again my memory gave a lurch and I stared at her, not answering when she said, 'He's so terribly clever, isn't he? Some of my scenes with John, they just made me *cry*.'

'You're going to write it for Beth?' Conway asked.

'If that's all right with you.'

'Sure it's all right with me. But just set it in s.w.3 if you don't mind.'

'Oh no,' Beth said. 'It goes on in the South of France. Well, we could *all* go. Think what ... fun we could have, the four of us.' She smiled at Jake with solemn eyes.

'Tell her,' Conway implored. 'You tell her. Women are made for bashing, and for having kids. That poor little girl of mine is lonely as hell. It's criminal, goddamit, not to have some more while the going's good. Look at you, you've got swarms of 'em, and from the glint in the old boy's eye tonight you'll probably have swarms more. She's always on about her figure. What figure, I ask her. Call that a figure? Flat fore and aft like a bloody paper doll. I bet your figure's better now than it ever was. Isn't it? Who cares about figures, anyway, but isn't it?'

'I don't know. I don't ...'

'You wouldn't say no to another one, would you? Not if your old man asked you?'

'Her old man,' Jake said, 'wouldn't be such a bloody fool. Let's have some more drink. Let's have some music. And Christ Almighty,' he plunged to the window and threw it open, 'let's have some *air*!'

'They remind me of someone,' I said.

'Who do?'

'The Conways.'

'They're two people. How can they remind you of someone?'

'I don't know ... My father's ill. I didn't tell you.'

'Oh, no. I'm sorry. What's the matter with him?'

'I don't know. I think it's cancer, but my mother won't say the word, she won't tell me.'

'Oh, I shouldn't think it's cancer. I'm sure it's not. It's probably just some ... bug or other. You mustn't worry.'

'I don't worry,' I said. 'It's just that ... you always say how much you like him. I remembered I hadn't told you.'

'Perhaps you ought to go down and see him?'

'She says only if he gets better, or if he gets worse. She wants to keep him to herself, I think. She loves him so much.'

'Well, that's good, isn't it? That's wonderful.'

I could feel his displeasure. Trust her, he was thinking, to introduce a jarring note. I should have kept this news of illness and sadness until tomorrow.

'I'm sure he's all right,' I said. 'Don't worry.' I got up from the dressing table. He was sitting, half undressed, on the bed. I knelt behind him, my arms round his neck. 'They've almost finished the tower.'

'Oh. Good.'

'You're a marvellous colour.'

'Well ... it was hot.'

'Do you think she's very attractive?'

'Who?'

'Who? Who? Beth Conway.'

'I suppose so. If you like that sort of thing.'

'Perhaps it's Philpot she reminds me of.'

He turned inside my arms. 'You love me, don't you?'

His eyes, as always, were expressionless, but his voice and body were warm. 'Yes,' I said. 'Of course I do.'

'You missed me,' he stated. 'You wanted me to come back.'

'Yes.'

'You're not disappointed in me.'

'Why should I be?'

'I behave stupidly. I do bloody stupid things.'

'No. You don't.'

'I love you. I need you. I want you. You're important to me, important to me.'

'Yes. Yes, I know.'

He lay down, pulling me with him. 'You're ... fixed up all right?' he asked. I didn't answer. In dreams you need no parachute, no wings; in dreams you can fly.

14

My father groped for my hands. I gave them to him and he lifted them, pressing them against his eyes. After a while his own hands dropped, but I didn't move. My mother was sobbing by the window, little squeaking sobs with no strength in them. I sat for a long time with my hands over my father's eyes, until my arms ached and I was afraid of leaning on him too heavily. When I drew them away, gently as quilts from a sleeping child, I knew he was dead.

'I think he's dead,' I said.

'Dead?'

'Yes. I think so.'

She ran to him, crying. I couldn't bear to see her touch him, holding him, persuading him back to life.

'Don't,' I said. 'Don't. It's no good ...'

'The doctor. The doctor ...!'

'Yes, I'll get the doctor.' I tried to lift her up. 'But come away.'

She shook her head, twisting it from side to side on his chest. 'George!' she called. 'George ...'

I went downstairs and telephoned the doctor. Then I went into the kitchen and put the kettle on. The kitchen was full of trays. For two days and two nights my mother had said, 'You must have a little snack, dear. Yes, I think I might have a little snack.' I tipped all the little snacks into the dustbin and emptied three teapots. My father is dead, I told myself cautiously. My father is dead. Somehow I felt that it should be a great statement, tragic, triumphant. My father is dead, long live ... That was for sons, though. He had no son. He had never needed me until that moment when he took my hands. A son's hands would have been hard, uncomforting. Perhaps he had been trying to say he was glad. Or perhaps, in those last minutes, barely alive, he had needed protection, a shield against some intolerable light. As I washed my hands under the kitchen tap and dried them, slowly, finger by finger, on the roller towel, I thought of all the things they had done; now they were mosses for a dead man's eyes. Familiar hands, very similar to his: broad-heeled, long fingered, square tipped, the skin already puckering on the knuckles, the wedding ring loose. They felt empty. The only sensation I had was of empty hands.

Late that night we sat in his study, my mother and I. They had been to lay him out and for hours, it seemed, the house had been full of their mournful tramping, their buckets, their winding sheets. ('Anything'll do, dear, anything nice and clean. An old table runner, now, that'd do very nicely'). They had left his windows wide open, and the house was very cold. He lay like a little man struck by a blizzard on the double bed with its clean sheets and unnecessary heaps of pillows. He was askew, but I hadn't the courage to straighten him out. The blowing wind and the smell of formaldehyde, the dark and the icy bed, frightened me against my will. We were snug, almost riotously snug, in the study. I had bought some brandy and my mother was slightly tipsy. Each time a door creaked we glanced up, but not at each other in case we should spread alarm.

'He was such a good man,' my mother said for the tenth time. 'Nobody knew how good he was. Well, look how he helped you and Jake to get started. Have you told Jake yet? He was very fond of George. There are many things I don't care for about Jake – I know I've never said so, and I hope I've never shown it. But he was very fond of George. And George was fond of him. George really *was* fond of him.'

'I know,' I said.

'He didn't care for any of the others, although he might have got used to the Major, if he'd lived. But Jake ... I don't know what it was, he was really *fond* of Jake.'

'Yes. Jake was fond of him, too.'

'I know he was.'

At last I got her upstairs. She wanted to sleep with me in my old room, so I tucked her into Ireen's bed. She began to cry again, but wouldn't take a sleeping pill. 'It's so terrible to think of ... his poor body there ... but he's gone, I'll never see him again ...'

I stroked her frizzed grey hair. Her face was sodden with tears.

'You don't believe in God, do you?'

'No,' I said.

'Neither do I. George never knew that, he would have been shocked, I think he would have been ... Do you?'

'No, I'm sure he wouldn't have been shocked.'

'I wish I did,' she whispered. 'Oh, I wish I could believe I'd see him again. You don't think ... it's possible?'

'Anything's possible,' I said.

'But not that. Oh George, George ...' She turned her face into the pillow. She was seventy, and hopeless, and I didn't know how to comfort her. I went to the window and drew back the curtain. It was too dark to see the church spire.

'Ma ...'

'I'm glad he wanted to be cremated. I *am* glad about that. It would be dreadful to think ...'

'Ma, listen.'

'To think of him buried ...'

I sat on the edge of her bed and held her shoulder.

'I want to tell you something.'

Automatically, obedient to years of training, she perked round, sniffing back the last rush of tears. 'Yes, dear?'

I swallowed, looked confused, not meeting her eye.

'No!' she said. *'No!'*

I nodded.

She sat bolt upright, almost knocking me off the bed. She scrubbed her face furiously, repeating again and again.

'You're not! You *can't!* My dear child, you *can't!*'

'Well,' I mumbled, picking at the fluff in the blanket, 'there it is ...'

'But it's insane! What can Jake be thinking of? What – ?'

'He doesn't know yet. You're the first person I've told.'

'But how *can* you start all that over again? How *can* you? My poor child, are you *never* going to get any rest? ...' I didn't have to listen any more. I knew it all by heart. Slyly, under cover of the barrage, I tipped two sleeping pills out of the bottle and reached for the glass of water. 'You'll be the death of me,' she said, using the word as though it had no meaning. 'You will, you'll be the death of me. Have you *no* consideration for other people? In my mother's day there was no proper prevention but how can you *contemplate* ...' In these moments of crisis, which she loved, my mother had great fluency. 'This! This on top of everything else! I'm glad your father didn't live to see it. Yes. I am. I'm glad your father ...'

'I'm sorry,' I said. 'I shouldn't have told you. Here, you'd better take these pills.'

She took them without noticing she was doing so. I pushed her gently back on to the pillow and straightened the bedclothes. She nagged me heartily all the time, her face pink with outrage. I turned out the bedside light.

'When will it be?' she asked.

'Oh, not for ages. Not till October.'

'October!' she groaned, her eyes closing. 'How *will* you manage?'

'We'll talk about it in the morning.'

'Careless girl. How could you be so ... careless ...'

She slept abruptly. I went downstairs and, sitting at my

father's desk, wrote to Jake. I told him that my father was dead and that to take her mind off it I had told my mother that I was pregnant. I said it had taken her mind off it wonderfully, so far; and that it also happened to be true. I said that I hoped he didn't mind too much, and that I was very happy about it myself. I asked him to see that the char was paid, and to give my love to the children, and told him that I would telephone his secretary about the cremation, it would please my mother very much if he could manage to come. I gave him my love, drew three children's kisses at the bottom and left it, with threepence, on the kitchen table for the postman to collect in the morning.

15

Jake drove down for the cremation, and he brought Dinah. I didn't know what to expect, although I knew that he wasn't going to burst into my mother's house and congratulate me. He walked straight past me and saluted my mother on both cheeks. Then, holding her elbow, he led her into the study.

'I don't know what's eating him,' Dinah said. 'He didn't speak the whole bloody way.'

'Don't talk like that in front of Gran. Please.'

'Sorry. He drove like a bloody maniac, too.'

'Oh, Dinah ...'

'He did. Is everyone very miserable?'

I hurried into the study. It was all right. My mother was going through the catalogue of my father's affections: '... I was just saying the other night, how fond he was of you, Jake. He was very proud of you, too, you know. Only last week, I can't believe it now, but only last week he said, "Mame, we must go and see that film of Jake's at the Odeon." Of course he hadn't been out for three months, but that seemed such a sign of hope. And now ...'

'Is there a drink?' Jake asked, not looking at me.

'Oh dear,' my mother said. 'There they are.' She began to cry again.

'We can't ... get to the front door,' the undertaker murmured. 'Could the gentleman please move his car?'

'Could you move your car?' I asked Jake.

I thought he was going to refuse, but he moved it.

'Could you see they get him down all right?' I asked. 'I'm going to take her into the garden. She doesn't want to see him go away.'

He didn't answer. Dinah and I walked my mother over the lawn, through the shrubbery to the vegetable patch. My mother, in her hat, was still weeping. 'He loved his vegetables,' she said. 'We never bought a single vegetable until this winter, when he couldn't manage it any more. Remember the strawberries, Dinah? You loved his strawberries.'

'Yes,' Dinah said. 'They were super.'

'He thought you were growing just like your mother – he meant when she was your age, of course ... Do you think they've ... finished now, dear?'

'No,' I said. 'Let's walk round once more.'

My mother blew her nose, then again clung to Dinah. We bent our heads against the wind and started round the sprouts again. 'She was a wild, harum-scarum little girl, though,' my mother said. 'What was the name of that friend you had to stay that summer? Eileen, was it? George liked her, I remember. What was her name?'

'Ireen,' I said uneasily. 'You could let this off for allotments, couldn't you?'

'Ireen. That's right. She wrote to your father, such a sweet letter. She said she wished her father was like *him*. George was so modest, he was quite angry with me for reading it. It only seems like yesterday, and now ... He didn't even say goodbye ...'

'Run and see if they're ready,' I told Dinah.

'Okay.' She ran like a woman, not a girl, with her knees together and her feet wide apart. Perhaps it was cruel, but I wanted to cry, to be sorry. Had she loved him? Did she love anybody? Did she even love me? What would she say when I told her that I was pregnant again? Would she think it … disgusting?'

'Don't say anything to Dinah. About the baby, I mean. You won't, will you?'

'Of course not, dear. But Jake knows, I hope?'

'Yes; Jake knows.'

'It seems so dreadful that he'll have a grandchild … after he's gone. He loved the children you know. Oh, he used to get angry, he used to say you had far too many. But he always loved them, you know that.'

'Yes,' I said. 'Come on, now. They're ready.'

We drove to Luton at ten miles an hour, my father in his disposable coffin leading the way. There was no ashtray in the Daimler, and each time Jake finished a cigarette he wound the window down and threw the stub out. My mother had at last stopped talking. I had never seen Jake so pale, haggard. He sat with his back to the undertakers, his coat collar turned up, smoking with short, savage puffs. Dinah kept coughing. I daren't say anything. My mother took my hand and held it tightly. At the crematorium there were a few relatives, all the office staff from the factory and three or four of the men; there were representatives from the Rotary Club, the Borough Council, and the British Legion. Dinah turned down Jake's collar and he gave her a weak smile. In the chapel I stood between Dinah and my mother, but I was only conscious of Jake. 'Fight the good fight,' my father's good friends sang, 'with all thy might, Christ is thy strength and Christ thy right …' Jake stood with his hands in his pockets. I felt that his hands and his teeth were clenched; that he was sweating. It could have looked like grief, but I knew that it was anger. 'Faint not nor fear,' the Rotarians sang, 'his arms are near, He changeth not and thou art dear …' My eyes burned with tears, but not for my father. My mother squeezed my hand. She was glad to see me crying at last.

The doors opened, the coffin and the wreaths moved slowly away into the efficient, unseen furnace. Dinah's eyes were wide, her lips parted, she was shocked. We knelt, and the clergyman began some droning prayer. 'Oh, why can't he be *quiet*!' my mother whispered savagely. I wished Jake could have heard this. I felt him looking at me and turned quickly. He stared at me. I smiled. He turned away, covering his eyes with his hand. I had been apprehensive, now I was frightened. I prayed, but not for my burning father. Let it be all right. Make it all right. Stop him looking at me like that.

Immediately we got home, he left, taking with him the bewildered and profanely protesting Dinah. My mother said, 'He seems so upset. I wish I could think it was because of George. But I suspect it's something *quite* different.'

16

To explain what happened between Jake and myself is impossible, I know that. We didn't love each other as most people love: and yet the moment I have said that I think of the men and women I have seen clasped together with eyes full of loathing, men and women who murder each other with all the weapons of devotion. There's nothing new under the sun and even I have read – well, in parts – *The Origins of Love and Hate*. This is something you can't find in your magazines, Ireen, though by now, if you're still alive, you may have learnt it.

One of the greatest differences between Jake and my other husbands is that they were all peaceful men capable of great physical exertion, but Jake is a violent man who wears a sluggard body for disguise. Sleepy, amiable, anxious to please, lazy, tolerant, possibly in some ways a little stupid: this is the personality he wears as a man in the world. His indestructible energy, aggression, cruelty and ambition are well protected.

Perhaps he should never have let me see them. At the point where I learned what I was fighting, loving, I knew that I was bound, in the end, to lose. I dispensed with the formalities of tenderness, pity, the ceremonial flattery that should go before disciplined massacre. I fought, I suppose, like a woman, uttering distracting cries, making false moves, hitting below the belt. I was incapable of giving up, and unable to escape. But I was no match for Jake. He went on loving me even after I was beaten, propped up with my wound wide open, emptied of memory or hope.

*

My mother began to be irritated by me: I put things in the wrong place, forgot the fireguard, was extravagant with the Quix. She was also melodramatic about my pregnancy, suggesting that I should drink more gin. It seemed to me that she had recovered sufficiently to be left. I had not heard from Jake since the cremation and although every midnight I went to the telephone determined to call him, I could never make myself do so. It was not that I was frightened of his anger: I would have welcomed it. I was frightened that he would not be there.

I telephoned Dinah and said I was coming back. She said thank goodness, it was all chaos. What kind of chaos, I asked eagerly. She didn't know. Everything was fine. She had become a Deist. Yes, since the cremation. They were all well, but hurry back, it's absolute chaos.

It was snowing in London. The house was empty when I arrived. I walked round it looking for signs of life. There were very few. The dolls, bears and horses lay in orderly rows, the diaries and Biros were neat on bedside tables, the gramophones shut up, books back in the bookshelves, even if they were upside down. In Dinah's room howling guitarists, a copy of *Honey*, Tindal and Voltaire. In the boy's room, Gagarin and Glenn, a half-built Meccano windmill. In the nurse's room, the electric fire left on and a dirty teacup with one cigarette stub in the saucer. In Jake's study, nothing: the typewriter covered, ashtrays clean, wastepaper basket empty. It was like walking into a stranger's house, or into a house left desolate by some plague. Who are these people? Who are these children of varying sizes and sexes? Do they feel, do they think, do they look forward to anything, do they remember? Are they happy? They had built snowmen out in the garden. They were an army, self-contained. I was suddenly frightened of them; afraid that when they came back they would find me here, trespassing, and judge me coldly. Across the gardens I could see a great bonfire built by the demolition men. Its flames leapt up, fed by mantelpieces and doors. It crunched them and spat them out, ravenous.

I went up to the attic. Snow had piled on to the skylight and I couldn't see without the light on. I hauled out a cot and a rubber bath. The rubber had perished and stuck together. There was a high chair and a pair of scales piled up at the far end of the attic, but I couldn't reach them without moving a dozen suitcases. I heard, far down in the house, the front door slam. I threw the cot and the bath back into the attic and shut the door. What would they think if they found me grubbing about up here? They would think that I had gone crazy.

When Jake and I were first married – after the three eldest children had been taken away – we lived together in the evenings. Like actors, our lives began when the curtain went down. We ate and quarrelled and made love, cooked and drank and talked through the night, while the audience slept. Then, beginning with Dinah, the children began staying up later. They needed help with homework. They needed food. They needed conversation. They needed more and more of our lives. In a useless attempt to keep something for ourselves, we gave them bed-sitting rooms, television sets, new electric fires; but at eight o'clock, then nine o'clock, then ten o'clock they would be sitting in a patient row on the sofa preparing to talk to us or play games with us or perhaps just watch us, their eyes restless as maggots, expecting us to bring them up. My guilt and Jake's exasperation loaded the atmosphere until, to me, it became unbearable. But the children breathed it in placidly. There were now more great bored ones staying up in the evening than there were small, manageable ones asleep with their teeth cleaned. The nurse went off duty, as she called it, at half past seven, seldom failing to remark that she had had a twelve hour day. We went out, in order to be alone, to the great dirty pub on the corner, to the cinema, anywhere where we might be anonymous and behave, if necessary, unsuitably to our age and situation. That night, after I came home, there was no question of going out. We waited, with bad grace and burning impatience, for them to go to bed.

At last, lingeringly, with sad backward glances at the glorious day, they went. They could well look after themselves, but because I had been away I went about picking up socks, opening windows, telling them to hurry, tucking them in. Encouraged, they clung to my hand, each jealous of another, demanding to know about death and sex and other subjects which they hoped might interest me. When one of them pestered unduly, another would demand that I was left alone; when one of them called for me to go back and listen, another said crushingly, 'You are a beast, can't you see she's tired.' By the time I left Dinah, dazed by the possibility of a Supreme Being, my longing to be alone with Jake had cooled and hardened into a longing to forget, to postpone, to sleep.

'I suppose you're tired,' he said, the first words he had spoken directly to me for nearly two weeks.

'Yes. I am.' I sat down, kicking off my shoes, stretching my toes. Under cover of this nonchalant gesture I looked at Jake. He, feeling it, looked at me. We both turned to the fire, as though to a third person.

'You look terribly tired,' I said.

'I am.'

'You look ... awful.'

'I feel awful.'

There was another silence. How many nights had we sat in this room testing, probing, waiting for the moment to strike? A year of nights, between Philpot and now? No, more than that. We were both nine years older, nine years more cunning, nine years more dependent.

'I'm sorry,' I said. 'I know you're upset. I know you don't want this baby.'

'Do you?' A look of such hope struck his face that he sat blinking, as though puzzled with it. In fact, I had not known. Perhaps I had even thought that by some miracle he might now be glad. I found that I was kneeling to him, holding his limp hands. 'I'm sorry. Darling, darling Jake, I'm sorry ...'

He said nothing.

I said, 'I know just how it feels to have got someone into trouble. This must be just how it feels. I've got you into trouble, haven't I?'

'It can't be helped.'

The weight of resignation in his voice made me desperate. If he had shouted, hit me, I could have fought back. But he was shutting me out, retreating into lethargy.

'It'll be all right,' I said. 'I promise you. You'll like it when it's born, you always do, perhaps it'll be a boy, you haven't got anything like enough boys, you haven't got as many as Giles even. One more won't make any difference, I promise you it won't. We'll have the tower ready and we'll spend the summer there. When we've got the tower we can spread out a bit, can't we, and you really won't notice it, Jake, I promise you ...'

'All right,' he said. 'It doesn't matter.'

'But it does matter! I can't have a baby you don't want!'

He looked at me sadly. He had gone. Something had stopped in him. 'You should have thought of that before,' he said, and almost smiled.

'You mean, you don't ... you *really* don't want it?'

'No.'

I knelt upright, humiliated by touching him. I got clumsily to my feet. I stood with my back to him, looking vaguely round the familiar room, the walls, maps of the time we had spent together, pictures, objects, things.

'What ... do you want, then?'

'It hardly matters, does it?'

'Oh. I see.'

By now I was used to fear. It no longer bewildered me as it had done the night Philpot left. Pounding heart, dry mouth, trembling, not a thought in my head but save me. But while it came and grew and I suffered it I knew that I was not at all afraid of what he had said; I was afraid of the reason for his saying it.

'Why?'

He hesitated.

'Don't work it out,' I said. 'Just tell me why.'

'Because I don't want it. That's why.'

'Yes. I see.'

The silences were the silences of a blackout in which actors run softly to take up new positions; they were longer than the tableaux in between, in each of which we were doing the same thing, but in different attitudes. I turned and faced him. 'But ... *why*?'

He sighed, looking at me. I suppose I looked absurd, shoeless, ravaged, demanding my answer with stiff hands. He patted the arm of his chair. 'Come here.'

'No.'

'I want to tell you the truth.'

'Then tell me the truth.'

'But come here.'

I went slowly. After a moment he began to stroke my hair as though I were a dog who had to be calmed.

He starts by saying that he is not a good person, like I am, but he doesn't say what he means by good. He says that he is weak, impatient and not to be trusted. He has done his best in the past, but even then he has failed me, dismally failed me. Does he believe this? Why this sudden humility? I want to believe it. I want to shut my eyes and be lapped by lies. Jake is humble.

He knows what's wrong with me. He's given me all the wrong things. Material things. He's neglected me. Perhaps this is true. He has never spoken like this before: rather too solemn, a bit pompous. He feels about this. He means it. Jake is trying to say something he means. Because of this short-sightedness of his, I came to feel my life was pointless and empty. Quite rightly. So it was. I was perfectly right to feel like that. And since he was no help to me, I took the only way out that I knew: I decided to have another child.

He is not blaming me. Jake is blaming himself. (Is he saying I didn't know any better? Well, if he is, it's true.) His first reaction was that he had been cheated. This, he says, is why he behaved so badly at the cremation. Then, after seeing me there, he began to think. Jake began to think. He thought it out and he realized that it was he who had cheated me. He had left me in a vacuum and I had simply grabbed what I could get, the only thing I could think of to make me happy again.

All right. All right, Jake. Go on. The fear is eased, the fire is warm, love is simple. Somebody is explaining things to me, understanding me. I'm resting now. I'll believe anything.

He isn't excusing himself, but he's been terrified by the task of supporting us all. For years he's been driven on by panic, taking on ghastly scripts he didn't want to do, accepting everything he was offered; destroying, incidentally, his own talent in the process, but that doesn't matter, the point is that he's kept us, we've come out of it alive. But the irony, the bloody irony of it is that just at this point when he has realized how much he loves me, when we could for the first time start planning a happier, more sensible life, just at the point when we could start thinking of a little *freedom* – I'm pregnant again. The whole thing starts all over. Instead of love and a good time – he doesn't of course mean a good *time*, he means a *good* time – and being able to go away together and see a bit of the world, broaden our horizons, enjoy what he supposes is our middle age – instead of all this, another child. To him, it's tragic. We could have lived so differently. But now . . . it's tragic.

Now he's stopped talking. The caves of the fire blaze with icicles, stalactites seen through tears. I don't speak, because he has something left to say.

Of course he knows, good God he *knows*, that the idea of abortion is repellent to me. It is to him, too. He would never dream of suggesting it. I must agree that he never has. It's only that the doctor, that psyche, did say that I shouldn't have another child. I'm in the middle of treatment, Jake says, for depression. An abortion would be perfectly legal. It wouldn't be underhand, nasty, anything like that. Still, he supposes that the only thing to do is to take the risk and have the baby and get down to work again. They want him to go to Hollywood for six months. He was going to turn it down, take the summer off. He had wanted to get to know the children again, he says; he wanted to take them out and dust them and polish up their faces. Now . . . oh well, that's life. Don't be upset, darling. Don't cry. I want to make you *happy*. Good God, after all, he's got me into this. All those boring months, the pain at the end. He only wishes he could get me out of it while there's still time.

I still say nothing. He is right. I believe him. But I can't say so. I feel myself like a torrent being dammed, being forced back, turned into new channels. I am a dead weight, like water.

He asks me if I love him. I nod, stupidly, a mute. He waits, stroking my hair again. In a little while I shall tell him that I shall do what he wants, that is more important to me than the child. But not yet. For a few minutes we will sit here, wondering.

This morning I got a letter. It was forwarded from a magazine that printed a picture of us last month, and a story about Jake taking up script-writing to keep the wolf from the door. It is written on blue paper and came in what I think they call a Manila envelope, such as they use for bills.

Dear Madam, it says,

I saw your picture in a book at the drs with all your wonderful children and read about your good luck in life. That is when I thought of writing in case you have something you can say to help me as I need some help badly and your face looks kind, I hope you do not mind this. I feel so terribly alone and so wrongly full of self pity that I had to write to you if only to get things off my chest, perhaps my letter will not reach you. I may not post it, but my life is so hard to live and such an empty place I feel I'd like to end it now. I am married with three children, all wonderful babies who I love dearly. Four months ago I had an Hysterectomy operation, I get up at 6 a.m. and go to bed about 9. My weekly wash for us all including a young boy who lives in I do in a copper boiler, the sort with fire beneath. I clean ten rooms a week, two toilets, cook dinner every day for the six of us as well as keeping my little ones happy, so I never get out for a night or get holidays. I'm behind in HP payments and get paid Saturday mornings, broke Saturday night. Perhaps I'm lucky compared to some but I feel so unhappy, tears fall so easy. My husband doesn't make love to me any more to make it seem worth while. Please write to me before I do something I'll regret because my love for the babies won't hold me here if things don't change.

> Yours faithfully,
> Meg Evans (Mrs)

P.S. I am sorry for the trouble but you didn't always have things easy so I was hoping you might know.

What should I say to Mrs Evans?

'Dear Mrs Evans, I enclose a cheque for £10. This, of course, is tax free and therefore worth double ...' 'Dear Mrs Evans, I am about to have an abortion and wonder if you could give me some advice ...' 'Dear Mrs Evans, We have a fine tower in the country, bring all the children and live in it ...' 'Dear Mrs

Evans, We all get what we deserve. I myself am not going to have another baby. Why not learn Italian or take up some useful . . .'

Dear Mrs Evans, my friend. Dear Mrs Evans, for God's sake come and teach me how to live. It's not that I've forgotten. It's that I never knew. A womb isn't all that important. It's only the seat of life, something that drags the moon down from the sky like a kite and draws the sea in and out, in and out, the world's breathing. At school the word 'womb' used to make them snigger. Women aren't important.

You have a vote, Mrs Evans. Now why don't you take advantage of it? I have a vote. Really, anyone would think that the emancipation of women had never happened. Dear Mrs Evans, let us march together to our local headquarters and protest in no uncertain terms. Let us put forward our proposals, compile our facts, present our case, demand our rights. The men – they are logical, brave, humanitarian, creative, heroic – the men are sneering at us. How the insults fly. You hear what they are saying, as we run the gauntlet between womb and tomb? 'Stop trying to be a man! Stop being such a bloody woman! You're too strong! You're too weak! Get out! Come back! . . .' When we were young, we said the hell with it and used our breasts as shields. But the tears fall so easy when they take away love. Be a man, Mrs Evans. It's all that's left for you.

'What's this?' Jake said. He glanced at the letter, taking it from me. 'Oh, one of those.' It drifted into the wastepaper basket. He put his arm around me. 'Not crying again?'

'No.'

'I saw the doctor. He thinks you're perfectly right.'

'Oh. Good.'

'He says there's no need for you to go and see him unless you want to.'

'I don't want to.'

'He'll write to this . . . gynaecologist. I've made an appointment for you tomorrow.'

'Thank you.'

'You're so brave. So splendid. It'll soon be over."

'I don't mind.' I held him tightly. 'So long as you're happy.'

'I'm very happy.'

While he held me, rather formally, in his arms I kept my eye on the wastepaper basket; it contained the only evidence I had in the world that I was not alone.

17

They not only terminated, as they called it, my pregnancy. They sterilized me, so that I should never again have to worry about having children. I consented to everything. Not only did I believe in Jake; I began very tentatively, to believe in myself. It was as though I were feeling my own face with my fingertips in the dark.

At first I lay for hours staring at the murky oblong of window to the left of my bed. I imagined all the other patients in the nursing home lying in the same attitude, their windows magnets for eyes set in barely moving heads. The wound didn't hurt, but for the first time in my life I could not move my body freely. To be cut open and sewn up makes one realize how much is contained inside skin and muscle: we're only stuffed with life, and can easily burst open. Jake was careful not to touch me, or to inquire too much. He came every evening on his way back from the studio, and stayed until they brought my hot milk and pills. He usually ate my dinner, since he was missing his own, and I wasn't hungry. He held my hand and we talked rather desultorily about his work, the tower, the children. We didn't talk about the future. He seemed to have exhausted himself. I was rather shy with him, as you are with someone with whom you have made love once, for a single time.

After a few days the nurses said I was more lively. Every

morning Jake's florist sent flowers. The room was crowded with flowers. There was a pale pink azalea from the Conways – with love from Bob and Beth – and a Japanese garden from John Hurst, complete with bridges. Flowers were cabled from Hollywood, New York and Rome: they all said with love, with fondest love, with much love, even those from people I had never met. I had the impression that Jake's world was wide open, longing to take me in, while mine was already disposed of, burnt up along with the garbage.

Every morning Jake's secretary came with magazines, books, letters. I was allowed to send her out shopping, if I needed anything. I had never really known her before, but now I began to realize that she, too, lived with Jake. 'Oh, Mr Armitage would snap my head off if I did that!... Oh, Mr Armitage – you can never tell what he's going to do next ... Well, Mr Armitage doesn't know what it's *like* getting up from Croydon every morning ...' She was a pale, anaemic girl with a great beehive of yellow hair and a boy friend in Insurance. Her mother suffered from dizzy spells, she never knew when they were coming on, sometimes she had to go racing back to Croydon in the lunch hour just to cope with one of her mother's dizzy spells. 'There's no one else to look after her, you see. It's the worry of thinking she can't get hold of me, that's the real thing. She may be ringing the office now, or she may be ringing your home, or Elstree. One of these days I think I may get back and find her dead. You'd understand, of course, but don't tell Mr Armitage. I've got to hold my job down, but I never know from one day to the next whether she'll ring and ask me to come back, or whether she won't be able to get me and I'll go home and find her dead.'

Dinah came to see me after school. She brought a small bunch of violets, their stalks twisted in silver paper. 'Though, gosh,' she said wonderingly, 'with all the others you've got ...' I said truthfully that I preferred the violets. I didn't know how to tell her why I was there, I didn't know what to tell her. In the end I told her nothing.

'It's a sort of ... womb thing, I suppose, isn't it?'

'Yes,' I said. 'Something like that.'

'Does it happen to everyone?'

'No, of course not.'

'Gosh, you know, it's hell being a woman. Look at men. They can do just what they like. It makes me *sick* when I think of men.'

'Does it?' I asked. I was seeing her for the first time as though she were static, complete, no longer part of a moving chain. I wondered if all the children would appear like this, in focus, their outlines sharp and permanent: the youngest for ever the youngest, with no one to bully or protect. They seemed much nearer to me than they had done for many years. I talked to Dinah about them. We analysed each one. Where Dinah found fault, I defended; where I criticized, Dinah said it would pass. She was still there when Jake arrived, and the nurses said oh well, they'd have to leave me for once, if I died in the night they'd take the blame.

'Hullo,' Dinah said. 'I haven't seen you for ages.'

'No,' Jake said. 'How are you, then? How's Trotsky?'

'That just shows how out of date you are. Of course if you ever got up in the morning, I might see you.'

'If you didn't leave for school at half past seven in order to get there at nine, I might see *you*. What do you *do*, anyway? It can't take an hour and a half to get from home to South Kensington.'

'It does,' Dinah said, 'if you don't happen to go by *Jaguar*.'

She left, and I said, 'Perhaps you shouldn't come here so much. You ought to see them. You ought just to see they're all right.'

'They'll keep,' he said. 'Anyway, I go straight home when I leave you.'

'Then why don't you see Dinah? It's early when you leave here. It's only ten.'

'She's always in bed or ... messing about in her room, or something.'

'Is she?'

'Yes!' he shouted suddenly. 'She is! Didn't I tell you so?'

'I'm sorry ...' For the first time, my hands moved involuntarily to my stomach. They lay over the hot dressing, the wound I had never seen. I watched Jake inspecting the flowers.

'Sorry I shouted,' he said. 'I'm tired.'

'It's all right.'

'Did you write to the Conways, thank them for this?'

'Yes.'

'Good. People like Conway ... you know, they're touchy.'

It was almost time to go home. I knew now that it was all right, that I could make life work again. Although Jake and I didn't talk about it, I was full of plans. I planned during the day, when I was alone. I had hated the nurse for too long: she must go. I would take back the children and in the summer we would live in the tower. I would live with Jake. I realized that for the first time in my life I could make love without danger. Danger? For the first time in my life I could make love. It was an amazing thought, as though I suddenly had the gift of tongues, the ability to fly. I could hardly contain my love, it ran out of my arms and eyes like lightning. 'Be careful,' Jake said, 'you'll hurt yourself.' I laughed till the tears came and it really did hurt. 'You're crazy,' Jake said. 'What's the matter with you?' 'Nothing. I love you. I've been such a *fool*.' He laid me back against the pillows. 'No,' he said, 'you've never been a fool.'

The next morning they took the stitches out. They came at the time that Jake's secretary usually arrived, so I told them to ask her to wait. I saw the wound for the first time. It was larger than I had expected, a long, blood-caked gash between my navel and shaved pubic arch. It was very ugly. They covered it with sticking plaster and said it would soon fade. I knew they were lying. A scar is what they call a distinguishing mark. It lasts for ever.

Jake's secretary was nearly an hour late. She literally ran into the room, her beehive tumbling; her mascara had spread so far that her face appeared to be covered in small footprints. 'It's happened,' she said, 'I wasn't in the office five minutes before they rang – she's been taken to hospital!'

'You shouldn't have come round here. Hurry. Get a taxi –'

'Well, I didn't know what to do, Mr Armitage told me to take his letters down to the studio, he won't be in the office today. It's having to hold my job, I can't do it, Mrs Armitage. I wondered if you could give them to him this evening? I'll have to phone him of course, I don't know what he'll say, he'll probably sack me.' She wept into a clenched handkerchief and burrowed in a briefcase with her free hand. I told her to leave the letters, whatever they were, on the table, gave her a pound for a taxi, promised to clear her name with Jake, asked her to ring me to say how her mother was. She ran off clutching her hair, a girl with a desperate problem. I telephoned Jake at the studio. He said, 'Blast the woman.'

'She can't help it, darling. Do be a bit kind.'

'There's a pile of work waiting for her down here. What am I supposed to do?'

'You'll have to borrow someone else. Is it awful?'

'One of the camels has got the 'flu and John's going round telling the whole camera crew that Doug ought to be directing TV commercials and Dante's got a temperature and Beth's still not back. What d'you mean – awful?'

'Not back from where?'

'She's been off for a week, God knows what's the matter with her. Well, see you tonight if I'm still alive.'

'Take care of yourself.'

I got up now, and walked about my room. I already knew it so well that lying in my bed with my eyes shut I could reconstruct it exactly, green-painted furniture with stencilled motif slightly chipped, basket chair with cretonne cushions, crack in the wall over the wardrobe (why do ill people need wardrobes?), squat taps in the basin polished every morning, locker with ink stain, Victorian commode, two strips of cretonne hanging from ivory rings over the window. There was nothing to do in the room but walk round it. I brushed my hair three hundred times, watered the azalea, cut off a few daffodil stems with a pair of nail scissors, looked out of the window. It was a freak March, they said it was seventy degrees. Dinah, excellent with news, told me that the tortoises had come out of their straw. I could only see a jagged chunk of blue sky and people far below in the narrow street walking hatless, their coats open. In a week's time the workmen would be finished and we could move into the tower. I was in love with Jake; it was a convert's love, passionate, wholly occupying. I sang as I pottered round the room. The nurse, bringing in my lunch, said, 'You sound chirpy enough, time we got rid of *you*.'

In the afternoons they drew the two pieces of cretonne, took away the pillows and told me to sleep. That afternoon I was excited as a child before a party. I couldn't sleep, I couldn't rest. I made a list: sack nurse, sort out things for tower, THROW AWAY, ring movers, get cleaners, Jake's shirts, get hair cut, MAKE CLEAN SWEEP. At the bottom I wrote: love Jake. When this was done I decided to pack, to save time in the morning. It didn't take very long. I was disappointed to find that I was tired now, the sticking plaster dragging and burning. I had used up half an hour of the afternoon. What to do now? The telephones were dead until four o'clock, the nurses resting more fervently than the patients. I had piled all the books on the table for Jake to take home this evening. There must be one I hadn't read. I got up and looked them over. No, I'd read them all. Idle, bored, I flipped through the pile of Jake's letters. A few of them were addressed to Mr. and Mrs. Jake Armitage, but I didn't bother to open them. There was a mauve envelope with large, scrawling writing, marked Personal. I threw it on top of the pile and got back into bed. Lying there, I watched the mauve envelope. After a while, I got out of bed and opened the letters addressed to both of us: circulars, invitations, nothing interesting. Then I ripped open the mauve envelope, tearing it carelessly with my thumb. The mauve paper was headed in mauve print: *Beth Conway*. An arrow from this heading pointed to two words, scrawled and underlined: *needs Armitage*. I thought very clearly, I don't want to read it. I think I sat down somewhere, on the bed or the chair. Anyway, I held the letter in my lap because it seemed too heavy to hold it up. The writing was like a careless child's.

Jake baby,

How are you honey lamb, are you still managing without me? I'm so terribly sorry, poor darling, but you know why and it can't be helped, I only hope we can keep going afterwards. How brave, courageous and tough you are to face it all alone. But then I always knew you had it in you. Tell old B. and everyone that I'll be back on Monday even if it's on a stretcher. Make it a double stretcher in that case. What ho!

Apart from going out of my mind with fright I'm beginning to feel better now, but they're talking about sending me to a head shrinker next week. It's not a head shrinker I want as well you know. I'm writing this out in the garden with the sun blazing down like the height of summer and I'm thinking of you and Tunis and the old Sunset Strip if we ever get there. It's so sweet of you to say how much you need me now, and I feel just awful to be adding to your worries and not soothing them away. But keep going, Jake baby, don't let your eyes stray to those luscious bits hanging around the set, they're no good when it comes to it as well you know. I'm saving myself for you like you told me, although it's pretty difficult (you understand!).

If you write again my love be very careful (as I know you always are) but sometimes Bob gets the post before me and he always reads my mail or should I say male. See you on Monday and then !!

Much love and kisses,

Beth

I went to the basin and was sick. I could feel the lips of my wound parting, as though my wound were laughing at me.

18

The tea shop, like many teashops, was called the Copper Kettle, but I doubt whether there was a kettle in the place. If you ordered tea it came black, in a glass with a raffia holder, and you sweetened it with brown sugar. They only served black bread. There was music, Italian twist, on tape. It was very dark, for which I was grateful.

'I've made it my business,' Bob Conway said, 'to find out a few facts about Jake Armitage. He's been bashing around for years, but I suppose you know that.'

'Bashing around?'

'Author's perks. He gets the ones the stars don't want. There's a pub quite near the studio – well, I suppose there are pubs quite near any studio. Pricey, I should think, for a couple of hours, but that wouldn't matter to him, would it?'

'I only wanted ... not to be the only person to know. If I'd gone on being the only person, Jake wouldn't have cared.'

'He certainly wouldn't. He rang her this morning, you know that?'

'Yes. He told me.'

'Oh. Well, he's been sending her flowers to the studio every day, right up till yesterday. You know *that*?'

'It's the florist. Jake never remembers to cancel anything. He never ...'

'Don't be daft, duckie. He's crazy about her. She told me so herself. He's mad about her.'

If you walk into a torture chamber and ask to be tortured, there's no sense in complaining at the pain. If you go up Sam's lane with Mr Simpkin, you have only yourself to blame if he assaults you. Pain and evil are there for the asking, nobody's going to protect you from them. Homilies on samplers, tracts of facts, legends inscribed on a dying soul, I knew them all.

'He doesn't love her,' I said.

'Love? What's love? It was Dante before this, it seems they were always necking on the set until she got fed up with him. He's not much good in bed, I understand. A bit on the small side.'

I knocked over the chair as I got up. He grabbed my wrist. Still holding it, he got up, came round the table, picked up the chair, forced me back into it. The wound screamed and I doubled up, my arm being dragged back across the table.

'I'm ill ...' I said. 'Please ...'

'You had an abortion, didn't you?'

I nodded.

'You know *why* you had an abortion? Because Beth's a good girl at heart, she would have left him. He made you have it, so he could keep Beth. It's a charming thought, isn't it?'

'Let me go ... let me go.'

'Be your age, then. Let's discuss this thing sensibly. We're both in the same boat, we need to get together.'

I drew my hand back; it felt broken.

'Now,' Conway said. 'Are you going to divorce him?'

I shook my head.

'Good. I'm glad to hear it. I don't give a damn about Armitage, but I care for Beth. As it happens, I love Beth. That may sound crazy to you, but it's the truth. I don't intend to lose her. I'm going to go off now and lay every woman I can find and I'm going to tell Beth every time I do it. I'm going to make her suffer, by Christ, she's going to hear the lot – when, where, how, how often, and let me tell you I'm no under-sized egghead, I know what I'm up to. But Beth, no, I'll leave Beth alone. I wouldn't touch her with a barge-pole, not if she took her pants off and came crawling ...'

'I'm going now.'

'Oh no, you're not. We haven't finished. If he ever rings her or sees her again, I'll fry him. You understand? I'll blast him. You'll tell him that.'

'No.'

'You'd better. He's not a grown man, your husband, he's a puking boy. He can't even lay a girl without the whole world knowing it. Beth says he made her sick with his slop. I made her swear on the baby's head that she was telling me the truth. I brought the baby in and I told her to swear on its head. That's how I feel about it. If he tries to get in touch with her, I'll *know*, you understand? So tell him to keep off.'

'You must tell him yourself.'

'I don't want to speak to him. I don't want to hear his pansy voice.'

'Is that all? I want to go.'

'Just one more thing. I'm checking on Beth, you see. She swears she's telling the truth, but I'm checking on her. If she can lie about one thing, she can lie about another. I could go and ask all the girlies at the studio, of course, but since you're here ...'

I stared at him. His hand crept across the table and climbed on to mine like a small, hot animal.

'Is it true that when he's in bed he likes to ...'

I was running and crying, my arm braced across my stomach. It was a one-way street, the pavement very narrow. Jake, oh Jake, where are you? Save me, I'm dying. I turned into a broad street and stopped running. A dark stain was spreading over the front of my skirt. I pulled my coat together and walked with small steps, trying to keep my body stiff. It's my own fault, my own fault. Everything's my own fault. I knew I was parting with reason because this senseless nagging, that it was my own fault, kept on in some part of my head that didn't exist. Now it was saying my name. I walked on, carrying my reason like a high, tugging balloon. It's your own fault, and then my name. Somebody took my arm, forcing me to stop. I looked very closely into a man's face, and he was saying my name.

'Giles,' I said.

His hand was still on my arm. He was looking at me. I watched pleasure change to bewilderment, bewilderment to

117

anxiety. He was kind and good, he always had been. Where his hand touched my arm suffering flowed to and fro, a mutual transfusion of pain. He began to speak, but I left him in the middle of what he was saying because I could not bear the pity that he was about to feel.

19

'It's not true. What more can I say? The man's mad, he just wants to hurt you. It's your own fault. You've brought the whole damn thing on yourself from the start.'

'Did you sleep with Philpot?'

'Oh Christ, why drag up that old thing again? It's centuries ago. It's ancient history.'

'Did you?'

'Yes, of course I did.'

'But you told me . . . that you hadn't.'

'That's right. I lied to you. What else do you expect me to do?'

'Was it here? In the house?'

'I suppose so. I can't think where else I would have slept with her.'

'Often?'

'Why keep torturing yourself? As often as we could, I imagine. What the hell does it matter now?'

'Nothing matters now, I suppose. And yet something does.'

'Of course something does. The future.'

'No. Not the future. The truth.'

'Can't you see? Before you knew the truth, we were happy. What's the good in ferreting out the truth all the time? It's always unpleasant.'

'Is it only lies that are pleasant?'

'Usually. That's why people tell them. To make life bearable.'

'Yes. I see.'

'This thing's only turned into a nightmare now you've seen Conway. Before that it was nothing. I suppose you realize I'd have to marry the girl if he divorced her?'

'Why?'

'I'd have to stand by her.'

'What about all the others? Didn't you have to stand by them?'

'There weren't any others!'

'How many?'

'I've told you! None!'

'How many?'

'Half a dozen. A dozen. I don't know. What does it matter, how many?'

'When you were away, or when you were here?'

'I expect it was when I was away! Does that comfort you?'

'Yes, if it's true.'

'Then it was while I was away. *I* don't give a damn.'

'Why did you marry me, Jake?'

'Because I loved you.'

'Why did you marry me?'

'I married ... a background, I suppose.'

'What do you think about marriage?'

'I don't think it exists, really. There are just human beings in situations they make for themselves. What do *you* think about marriage?'

'What do you think about human beings?'

'That they're sad. And lonely.'

'Is that all?'

'Pretty well all ... Giles rang today while you were out. You know – your husband. Giles. He said he'd seen you.'

'Yes. We met in the street.'

'He asked if you were all right. He said you wouldn't speak to him.'

'That's right. I didn't speak to him.'

'Why?'

'I ... didn't know what to say.'

'Well, it's a bit odd when he rings up after God knows how many years – '

'Thirteen.'

'To ask if you're all right. I should have thought you'd fling yourself into his arms and ask him to take you back, considering how much you hate me.'

'I don't hate you.'

'Of course you do. Otherwise you'd never have told Conway.'

'I wasn't thinking about you. I was thinking about myself.'

'That's honest, anyway. That's the truth.'

'Why did you go to bed with her?'

'Oh, for God's sake.'

'Why?'

'Out of curiosity. Vanity. Wanting to keep young.'

'Did you love her?'

'I found her ... appealing.'

'But did you love her?'

'I love you. I don't know what it means, love.'

'Didn't you ever, any of the times ... try not to?'

'You know I have no self-control.'

'When I was in the nursing home ... didn't you mind?'

'Of course I minded! Good God, I came to see you every evening, didn't I?'

'And sometimes you went to her afterwards. Sometimes she had an excuse for Conway and met you, after you had left me.'

'It's not true.'

'Where did you meet? Somewhere near the nursing home? Would she be waiting for you there?'

'It's simply not true.'

'How many times?'

'Only a few times. She was ill too. She couldn't go out much.'

'Where did you meet?'

'A hotel, of course. Where do you think we'd meet?'

'Near the nursing home?'

'Not very far. I don't *know* where it was. Anyway, it never happened. What are you doing? What's the point of it?'

'Did you sign the register?'

'No!'

'You mean there are hotels where you can go for some hours, without signing the register?'

'Yes, if you pay! Good God, why don't you find out for yourself, if you want to know these things! Why ask *me*, of all people?'

'You sent flowers to her yesterday.'

'Yes. I sent flowers to her yesterday. Now I've cancelled the order. Why don't you shut up? Why don't you *die*?'

'How should I die?'

'I don't know. I don't care. Why don't you leave me?'

'We can't seem to leave each other.'

'No. I wish to God we could.'

'If you'd let me have the baby –'

'That was your decision. You decided that of your own free will.'

'But it didn't help either of us, did it? We both had our reasons. We both failed.'

'I don't know what you're talking about. Don't talk about it. I can't stand any more.'

'So what shall we do?'

'Forget it. I love you. I've always loved you. Forget it.'

'He says that you love her. He says that you made her sick with your ... love.'

'Well, it's not true. What more can I say? The man's crazy, he just wants to make you miserable. It's your own bloody fault, opening letters, talking to people. You've brought the whole damn thing on yourself.'

'Was Philpot the first, or were there others, before?'

'No, of course there weren't any others.'

'How many? Who were they?'

So we were back at the beginning again. There was no end. You learn nothing by hurting others; you only learn by being hurt. Where I had been viable, ignorant, rash and loving I was now an accomplished bitch, creating an emptiness in which my own emptiness might survive. We should have been locked up while it lasted, or allowed to kill each other physically. But if the choice had been given, it would not have been each other we would have killed, it would have been ourselves.

20

Now I realized how completely I had been absorbed by Jake. I needed the outside world, but had no idea where to find it. For the first time, I needed friends; there were none. Over-indulgence in sexual and family life had left us, as far as other relationships were concerned, virginal; we said we had friends much as schoolchildren, busy with notes and hearts and keep-sakes, say they have lovers. In a packed address book there was not one person to whom I could speak or write. If you have ever found yourself in this predicament, Ireen, and if you have followed your faith, you will of course have taken a part-time job, a cookery course, you will have plunged into bridge or spiritualism. Don't think I despise you. On the contrary. I envy you at last. I only knew how to do one thing, to give myself away. Now there was nothing left to give. It is a moral tale, proving that it is better to take life in neat steps and small sips than it is to believe, as I did, that there is a wealth which is perpetually renewed.

The wound would not heal. I had injections, pills, I was plugged and probed, my body, which had always done exactly as I wanted, turned spiteful. I became morbidly ashamed, avoided seeing myself naked, undressed in hiding. The idea that I was in some way monstrous grew unchecked, except by the feeble attacks of my own reason. Jake made love to me, for comfort, after the terrible evening battles; afterwards, while he slept, my thoughts were so hideous that when they became dreams I was consciously relieved and said to myself, as though under anaesthetic, this is only a dream.

I wanted to go home, but now my father was dead there was no home to go to, only a house where my mother mourned and thanked goodness that I had at last seen reason. Jake told me that he had heard that Conway was roaming London blind drunk. I knew this, because for a week after our meeting he had rung me every day with such vile punishment that now I never answered the telephone, and if I was alone in the house took the receiver off the hook. I began drinking because the thought that I was drinking gave me a kind of identity: each time I poured myself a brandy in the deserted afternoon I could say to myself 'I am a woman who drinks'. It was the positive action rather than the brandy itself that gave me courage. By tea-time I could sit at the head of the table and listen calmly enough to the children, even though I could not understand them. They roistered like billeted troops, cramming themselves with bread and chocolate, swigging great mugs of milk and sweetened tea, miraculously innocent, strong, indifferent. The thought of this half a ton of hungry, growing, sentient body and brain coming from my body should, perhaps, have satisfied me. In fact, lacking now my own instincts, values and beliefs, I had nothing to offer them, and what they offered me – dependence, love, trust – seemed a monumental responsibility which I could no longer bear.

The tower was finished. When we went there it looked bleak and foolish, like a monument to a disgraced hero, a folly built for some cancelled celebration. However, we dutifully filled it with furniture, with kittens that the children had found in a hedge. We made it work, because we had money. At home, in the shabby, dying house that my father had set us up in, the past was never entirely forgotten. In the tower there was only the future. We abandoned it, saying we would return in the summer. In the meantime we employed women to keep it clean, as one might employ cleaners for a sepulchre in which one hopes to rest, at some distant date, in peace.

21

'We thought it would be rather fun,' the young man said, 'if you told us what you think about the Bomb. I mean, you do have all these children, don't you?'

'Yes,' I said.

'That's splendid.' He settled himself a little more easily into the sofa. I felt that he had not been absolutely certain that this was the right house. 'I was so sorry to hear you'd not been well.'

I lifted a cigarette out of the box on the desk, read the brand name printed round the top – Jake now smoked Gauloise – and shut the lid of the box carefully.

'How did you hear that?'

'Your husband's secretary told me. On the telephone.'

'You telephoned?'

'To make an appointment. The secretary said – '

'That I was always in in the afternoons?'

'Yes. That's right. She said you were always here in the afternoons.'

'You told her ... what you wanted?'

'But naturally.'

I lit the cigarette and looked out of the window. In the next garden but one, a woman was hanging washing on the line; dust from the partially demolished house on her other side would blow on to her washing. Twelve years ago, you know, there were many ruins round here, willow herb grew in the remains of dining-rooms. Then the houses were rebuilt, their scars were patched, skirtings, spandrils, treads and risers washed, prepared and painted, sashes and beading renewed, soffits, reveals and sills replastered, slates and flashing replaced and repaired. All the garden walls were built again for neighbours to lean against and children to run on over the new ramblers and virginia creeper. Only last year I could look out of the window and see nothing but gardens, Pakistanis drip-drying their shirts, children swinging, typists lying in the sun. Now, as I looked, an entire wall tottered and fell. The woman at the clothes line hesitated for a moment before reaching for another clothes peg from her apron pocket.

I wondered whether it was worth telling the young man that where those straight houses had stood, holding families and 'cellists and old, exhausted Jews on every floor, they were now building cottages for company directors, with glazed front doors and wrought-iron shoe-scrapers. Would he think it was fun? I looked at him and he said, 'Anyway, I hope you feel better now.'

'Thank you. Yes.'

'How long have you been out of hospital?'

'About six weeks. But it was a nursing home.'

'It sounds much comfier.' He smiled hopefully over the back of the sofa, screwing himself round, since I was standing behind him.

'I'm sorry,' I said. 'I didn't ask you if you smoke ...'

'No. No, I don't, thank you.'

I walked over to the fireplace, so that he could straighten himself out. He was very young indeed: probably about the same age as my eldest child. He stroked his small camera tenderly for a moment, then said, 'Of course my own view is that it does us a lot of good to live in a state of insecurity. I'm all for it.' He waited, it seemed to me eagerly, but I didn't answer. His face clouded like a boy whose firework has failed to go off. 'Doesn't that make you angry?'

'If I were fifteen years younger, or you were fifteen years older, it would make me angry. As it is ...' I tried to smile, but he was bitterly offended and bridled, girlish. Oh well, he was longing to say, if that's what you think! I was sorry to have hurt him; he, after all, had done me no harm. I sat down, scraping at a bit of plasticine embedded in the chair with my thumbnail.

'I'm very frightened,' I said. 'Not for myself. I don't mind for myself.'

'For your children.'

'Of course.'

'Why?'

'Why?' I asked. But he looked back at me with perfect calm, unsmiling, his hands hanging between his narrow thighs, his toes pointed outwards, the upper part of his body concave, relaxed as a tramp on a park bench. 'Well ...' I said. 'For them it will be ... For them ... If they survive ...'

'You mean Strontium 90,' he said, 'and all that jazz.'

'Yes.'

'But you *know* that's all wildly exaggerated. Remember that scare last year? I mean you're not worrying about the *milk* or anything, are you?'

I nodded. I was worrying about the milk, about my children falling in love, about the creatures who crawled through the dark towards us, their ancestors, their loving assassins, breathing 'Why?' like a cold wind. 'Yes,' I said. 'I worry a bit about the milk.'

'And what do you do about it?'

'Nothing,' I said.

His expression was pleased. I stopped looking at him and said, working at the plasticine, 'It's like everything, isn't it? ... If you're a Christian you can ... put your affairs in order. I suppose you can be kinder to everyone. Be loving. Try to make your soul perfect. Try to make everyone happier.' I glanced up at him, keeping my head down. His face was stony. 'But if you're not, then you can either eat and drink and be merry or just ... go on living with it. But you have to change.'

'Do you?'

'Of course. It's a different ... climate. You have to change.'

He disliked me now. 'And how have you – changed?'

I threw a grain of plasticine into the empty grate behind the electric fire. 'You should talk to Dinah,' I said. 'She paints Ban the Bomb on everything.'

'Dinah?'

'My – one of my daughters.'

'How old is she?'

'Seventeen.'

'Oh, well,' he said, 'at that age ...' He was about twenty-three. 'I suppose she sits down all over the place?'

'No. She just paints Ban the Bomb. And wears a badge of course. She was a Deist, but there's no badge for that. It makes a difference.'

'You ought to approve of her, feeling as you do.'

'I do approve of her. If they had badges for being against ... capital punishment or the colour bar, or badges for protesting about there being no houses for people to live in – '

'She'd wear the lot, I suppose.'

'Certainly.' I was tired of his unshakeable middle age. 'She also belongs to a number of fan clubs.'

'Does she, indeed?'

He lifted his camera, aimed and shot. I heard Josephine, the new nurse, coming down the stairs. She tapped on the door and only after I had called 'Come in' was my youngest child, my last child, allowed to enter. She walked two feet, the extent of her leather reins, and the nurse said, 'Say good-bye Mummy,' from outside the door. This nurse would not come into what she called the drawing-room except by request. The little girl looked at the young man and her harness tinkled like Christmas. He swivelled round and shot her over the back of the sofa. She blinked and looked for the nurse, who tugged her gently backwards.

'And how old is this one?' the young man asked.

'Four.'

'We're just four,' the nurse sang, invisible. 'Just four, aren't we?'

The child swayed about on the end of her tether and scratched her angora bonnet with a mittened fist. Whatever she wanted to do, walk or scratch or keep quiet or pee at irregular hours, she was prevented. My mother thought her a dull child.

There was nothing wrong with her except her upbringing and the fact that she believed me to be always ill.

'Good-bye,' I said. 'Have a nice walk.'

'Where are all the others?' the young man asked.

'At school.'

'But there are some ... older?'

'Yes.'

'Where are they?'

'They're ... away.'

'In view of your feelings about the bomb – forgive me, but it's quite a point – will you have any more? Children, I mean.'

'This is a picture of the tower,' I said. 'We built a ... tower in the country.' I took the photograph from the mantelpiece and gave it to him, commanding him to take it. There it is, a permanent, indestructible and freehold tower, built for our grandchildren to laugh at in their middle age. There were heaps of rubble in the foreground, we were keeping it to grind into hoggin for the paths. Against fast-moving clouds the tower seemed to be falling, but in the picture the clouds were frozen into white puffs and the tower stood straight, closed, complete, like an unopened crocus. He glanced at it briefly.

'Very interesting. What made you build a tower?'

'I don't know. We couldn't buy much land. We had a lot of people to ... It goes up and up, you see.'

'Your local council must be very enlightened.'

'There are lots of towers about. Bell towers, watch towers and so on. It's not very enlightened really.'

'You go there at the week-ends, I take it?'

'Yes. We shall. It's only just finished. We shall be there all summer.'

I put the photograph back on the mantelpiece. I didn't want him to ask me any more questions. The telephone began to ring and he brightened up, looking at it eagerly as though it were speaking to him.

'Your telephone,' he said.

'I'm sorry.'

'No, go ahead. Go ahead. I'll take some pictures.'

If I had been alone, I wouldn't have answered it. I lifted the receiver slowly. The young man sat on the floor and shot up at me.

'Hullo?'

'Mrs Armitage, please.'

I panicked. The camera clicked and whirred. 'No. She's not here. I'm afraid she's out.'

There was only the slightest hesitation. 'That's you, isn't it?'

'I don't know what you mean.' The young man was staring at me, his mouth loosely open. 'Mrs Armitage is – '

'All right. Give her a message. Tell her Beth Conway's pregnant.'

I was looking into the little black hole of the receiver; it was full of grains of tobacco and dust. I heard Conway's breathing, rasping, regular.

'I'll ... tell her.'

'It's not mine. I thought she might be interested.'

I sat down, holding the receiver in both hands. The young man was up on the window sill.

'You'll get rid of it,' I said.

'Oh, no, Mrs A. Oh, no. I'm not giving her that pleasure.'

'What?' The young man darted forward and held a light-register against my face.

'She's going to have this kid in a public ward and if there's any way of stopping her getting a whiff of gas, I'll find it. She's going to wipe its bottom and stare at its ugly mug for the rest of her young life. There's going to be no more movies, no more champagne, no more hair-do's, no more sexy clothes for my little Beth. This kid's going to kill her. I've told her that. This kid's going to make her curse Jake Armitage for the rest of her days. I'm going to see that this kid turns her into an old hag, and if you saw her now you'd know that's not too difficult.'

'No,' I said. 'No. You can't – '

'So you want her to get off scot-free, do you? You're on the forgive and forget jag in the Armitage household. Well, I'm no fool. She'd be off with him again in a couple of weeks.'

'No – ' The young man was machine-gunning me from the end of the room. I turned my back on him, huddling over the telephone.

'Or someone else, then. I'm fixing it so she's harmless, you understand? I'm going to make her learn typing and work for it. She's going to hate that kid almost as much as I shall. How's that for justice?'

'Is there anything ... you want us to do?'

'Tell your bloody husband to keep out of my way, that's all, or by Jesus – '

I put the receiver down. The young man asked loftily, 'Is anything the matter?'

'No. No. Of course not.' I couldn't look at him. I couldn't breathe. For the first time I understood the meaning of impossibility. 'Is there anything else you want to ask me?'

'I don't know, really.'

'Then perhaps ...'

He remembered just in time. 'Would you,' he asked, 'keep cyanide capsules in your medicine cupboard?'

I turned to him. I didn't remember what he was talking about. I shook my head.

'Then really you would sooner feel that your children were suffering than dead?'

'Nobody ... would keep cyanide in a medicine cupboard.'

'But would you kill them,' he demanded impatiently, 'if they were certain to be maimed for life?'

'Maimed?'

'Mentally or physically injured. For life.'

'I think any child ... any child ... would be better off ... dead.'

'I thought,' he said, 'that you might.' He snapped his camera shut. 'And does your husband share that view?'

'What view?'

'Your pessimism.'

'I don't understand.'

He strangled his fist in the camera strap. 'Your attitude to the *bomb*,' he croaked, and cleared his throat.

'No,' I said. 'Jake believes that we must live on the assumption that we are going on living. Jake believes in the inevitability of life.'

He stared at me for a moment, openly; then his blank eyes slowly filled with thought. He was seeing himself on his way, bowling through the park in his Mini-minor, beautifully smiling at old ladies on zebra crossings; whistling, probably, to keep his spirits up. Holding the camera in both hands, he sprang athletically to his feet.

'Well,' he said, 'it was extremely kind of you to see me.'

'Do you think life's inevitable?' I asked.

Now it was he who said, 'I really don't know,' hurrying out because he thought I was mad. I got up and followed him down the hall. He opened the front door and started down the steps, running sideways.

'Do you think life's inevitable?' I asked.

He was out of the gate, plunging head-first into his little scarlet car.

'Do you think life's inevitable?' I shouted.

The car spat away like a red hot cinder. A small boy stopped in the gateway; he watched me steadily, still as a cat. I looked at him from the top of the steps. He had pale blue eyes and red hair and was clutching a brown carrier bag; his shorts were two skirts over his fat knees. I moved as though to attack him, suddenly. He ran away very fast, wailing up the empty street like a coward.

22

'I'm so glad you came to me.'

'My dear *Giles*, there wasn't anywhere else to go. How do you like that? Fourteen years and nowhere to go, like someone coming out of gaol. Now you're sorry for me, but you won't be for long. I know that ... I bet you that within half an hour you'll have stopped feeling sorry for me. No, I'll tell you why. I will tell you why. Because you can't keep being sorry for people who don't know what's going on. And I don't know even *now*. Things happen. I look. I'm miserable, or frightened, or angry. But up here, in my head, I do not know what it *is* that's happening. I can't *believe* what is happening. Always there's a voice that says it's not true, people are good, kind, reasonable, loving, all this is just a dream, I won't be made to accept it, I'll be able to wake up. If you can't believe facts you don't care about them, if you can't care about them you can't change them. But the thing that stops you believing must be ... such smugness, such conceit.'

'If you don't believe that all this has really happened, why did you come here?'

'If I had believed it, I wouldn't have come. I would have been able to change it, somehow. This doesn't change anything.'

'Nothing?'

'No, of course not. I'm very ... grateful to you. But, you know ... I can't even believe this, Giles. I know it's true. I left the house, just after that boy ran away, after I'd made him cry. I drove down here and I waited in the car for two hours till you came back. I remember it, but it's like remembering seeing a woman sitting in a car. Then we came up here and you gave me a drink ...'

'Yes.'

'I had a lot of drinks.'

'Yes.'

'And I told you ... I suppose I told you about ...'

'You told me about the Conways, about the operation.'

'Yes, of course. You see, I don't remember what I told you. I only remember what we did. I asked you to come to bed with me.'

'Don't you believe that?'

'I believe it, but I don't believe in it. It's not really happening, I kept saying to myself. It's not really true. As though while I was telling myself that, I needn't really be involved. Oh Giles ... I'm sorry. Can't you make me believe something's real? Can't you make me?'

'Obviously not.'

'I've won my bet.'

'I never took on any bet. You can't stop me feeling sorry for you.'

'But I don't want you to feel sorry for me. It humiliates me.'

'Then I'm sorry for that. I'm no good at fighting. I never was. Is that what you need now?'

'I don't know. Maybe it is, but that's something else I can't believe. I feel ... I want ... I need what we had, in those years in the barn ... And yet it was always falling down, and the noise. You never once lost your temper. The children made the noise, but we were quiet. Sometimes I try to remember the evenings, but what did we do? Did we talk to each other?'

'Yes, I think so.'

'What about?'

'I don't know. Whatever people talk about.'

'I can't remember. Did we quarrel?'

'No. You just said, I never lost my temper.'

'Why? Are you so good?'

'No. I'm lazy, rather timid. You had your own way over everything.'

'Is that true?'

'Of course.'

'But didn't you mind? Didn't you ever think I was wrong?'

'Sometimes. But you had such a belief in your own infallibility that it would have meant ... Well, I hadn't the courage.'

'It seems to me we were so happy.'

'We were. At least, I was. Your belief in yourself made me happy. It was like a great tide I could be carried along on. Very strong and natural, and it seemed to me pure.'

'But if it was flowing in the wrong direction? If it was just ... chaos, really?'

'Tides can't flow in the wrong direction. It's an impossibility.'

'I mean, you let me believe that life was as easy as that? You knew it couldn't last. I was bound to find out sooner or later. We were so alone there, but one day the outside world would have come breaking in –'

'It did. Jake.'

'It had to be someone, or something. The children would have grown up and stopped believing in me. So would you, at some point, because ... anyway, there were other things.'

'I couldn't keep you, that's all. You didn't need me. At least Jake's managed to keep you up to now, although Christ ...'

'What? What's the matter?'

'Nothing. Does it hurt if I touch it?'

'No.'

'You believe this is true, anyway?'

'Yes. I do. If I didn't believe in that, I'd really be mad, wouldn't I?'

'You were mad to let them do it.'

'But I thought it was the first really sane thing I'd ever done. Only I did it for the wrong reason, I thought ... How can you tell about anything? It's what you do that matters, the reason is just ... nothing. The reason why Jake and Beth Conway went to bed together – whether it was good or bad, it couldn't matter less. Reasons don't have consequences, only actions. She's pregnant and I'm sterile. I'm in bed with you, and who cares if it's justified or unjustified? I'm in bed with you, and Jake and the children don't know where I am. I could ring them up and tell them why, but what difference would it make? You may feel you're right or wrong in killing someone, but the result is, they're dead.'

'Put my dressing-gown on. You'll get cold.'

'Shall I make tea or something?'

'No, I'll make it.'

'I'd like to make it.'

'Perhaps you'd better go back.'

'Do you want me to?'

'I just want to help you. It's time someone helped you.'

'You mean you're advising me?'

'I don't know. You're thinking about the children.'

'No, I'm not. They're perfectly well looked after.'

'Don't talk like that!'

'You almost shouted. Why? Don't you believe me?'

'No. You've been hurt, you're confused. But you love the children.'

'You sound like someone reciting a kind of creed. Supposing I told you that I didn't love the children, that I don't give a damn about the children? It might be true, you know. But for years you've relied on me to bring them up and provide love and cut their fingernails and teach them to tell the truth, as though it mattered. You've been free. Supposing I want to be free?'

'That was the way you wanted it then. I don't believe you've changed so much.'

'Then you're like me, not believing what you can see and hear, not even believing what you feel.'

'The kettle's boiling.'

'You've relied on Jake, too. He's kept them, he's even been fond of them. No wonder you tell me to go back. I can't think why you ever let me stay.'

'The tea's ready. You bring it in. I'll light the fire.'

'There must come a time in your life, mustn't there, when the most important thing to do is to find out who you really are, what you're really like. That doctor I went to ... he made me angry, he wanted me to change. You know, he wanted to sterilize my ... *attitude* to everything. All right, it was an idiotic attitude – that you have a kind of duty to avoid ... evil. I couldn't even tell him what I meant by evil. I kept on talking about the dust ... I don't know what to do, Giles. You think I should go back?'

'Not if you don't want to.'

'I don't know who I am, I don't know what I'm like, how can I know what I want? I only know that whether I'm good or bad, whether I'm a bitch or not, whether I'm strong or weak or contemptible or a bloody martyr – I mean whether I'm fat or thin, tall or short, because I don't *know* – I want to be happy. I want to find a way to be happy, I don't care what it is. You see, everything I say sounds absurd. Like a child talking. I don't even believe it myself. You know, one night, before all this happened, I was alone in the house.'

'Alone?'

'Jake wasn't there. Perhaps he was still abroad. I can't remember. Anyway, I was alone.'

'Yes. I see.'

'It was about half past eight. It was the cook's night out – I mean the night when she doesn't come, because she doesn't live in – and Dinah had the 'flu or something. Anyway, she was in bed and I was cooking leeks. I remember because of the smell, it filled the whole house. You know the smell of leeks – strong and sharp, but sweeter than onions, very like sweat. It's a reek, really, more than a smell. I like it very much. Anyway, I was wondering how to get through the evening. The leeks were cooking and the children were in their rooms and the nurse – oh yes, the nurse had just given notice, she did that once a month, but in the end I sacked her and got another. Although in the middle ... there was a short time in the middle when I didn't think I would get another nurse. She had gone out too. That nurse went to all the new plays because she had a friend who worked in a ticket agency. She was always amazed by them. "I'm amazed," she used to say, "that people go to things like that." As though it were my fault. Anyway,

I was alone, and since it didn't matter, I was talking to myself a bit. At the end of the day, if Jake's away, I forget what words sound like. I suppose I was giving myself another drink and telling myself the time and asking myself what was on television. I don't know, but what I do know is that I was ... well, I was despairing. This was before I met you again. You know how silent London can be? At the tower there's usually noise – I don't know, the rooks, the lambs, the cows, the dogs, they kick up the most terrible racket, even in the dark. But in London, where we are, when the demolition men have stopped, there are great long times of silence. Then a lorry goes up the side road, or a car; or a train, somewhere miles away. You know people are going somewhere. You try to imagine where they're going. You try to imagine the people, but they have blank faces, only they all lean forward in the same eager attitude and they all seem to be young. You imagine them whizzing about, from place to place, never still, never alone. They go round the house with a great tearing noise and then they've gone, and there's silence again. That wasn't an extraordinary night, I mean nothing had happened to make it particularly unbearable.'

'I thought you must have friends, hosts of friends.'

'The doorbell rang so I walked down the hall in the dark, and turned on the light and through the glass I saw this Jamaican. He was wearing a camel-hair overcoat, he was rather handsome, about forty, with a beard. When I opened the door I saw that he had something written down the front of his overcoat in red paint. He said he was glad I wasn't frightened or alarmed, and that I might like to know that he was the new King of Israel, anointed by Yahweh, the Eternal Lord God, and that he had come to give me his blessing. I thanked him and he talked for a time about the Emphasized Bible and how the name Yahweh appeared well over seven thousand times in the Emphasized Bible and how he had been appointed to fulfil some prophecy in Ezekiel – and this appeared seventy-two times, I think. I didn't really listen, but I thought why shouldn't he be King of Israel? Why not? And why shouldn't Yahweh have anointed him, and why shouldn't he bless me? I gave him five shillings to build a radio station in Jerusalem and he said, "The people are unhappy because they give the gift of their love to unworthy men and unworthy women." '·

'And then?'

'Then he went away, I suppose, to eat on the five shillings.'

'But he was a maniac.'

'He didn't seem like a maniac. I'm not saying he was sane. But neither was I. I'm not saying he even believed in himself, but neither did I. He got five shillings from me and I ... I was comforted. I told you I don't know who I am or what I'm like, but I know there aren't any rules – perhaps the kind of person I am believes in Yahweh. Perhaps that Jamaican King of Judah and I need the same thing. Anything's possible. When I was young – well, you remember – I thought that to need comfort was humiliating, that it was sufficient to be alive, and make love, and have children, and behave as well as possible. Well, it was sufficient. Now these things have been taken from me, but not naturally. I don't know, and now I never will, but I imagine that the natural way is gradual, that you're given time, that you're old enough to accept it, even with relief. What happened to me was sudden and artificial and it was done by people – oh, and by me, of course; I did quite surely to myself what I would never have done to anyone else. But that cruel truth people tell when they're meant to be comforting someone – the nurse keeps saying it to the children when they fall off a wall or lose something they love or run out of pocket money – "You have only yourself to blame!" It's far worse of course than being able to blame someone else. "Only yourself," is terrible. That is what Conway is saying to her. I know. Like a torturer, over and over for the rest of her life, "You've only yourself to blame." What are the good of such judgements once something has been done?'

'She gets the worst of it. Beth Conway. She's the worst off.'

'Yes. I know. But ... there is a kind of hope for her. She

may ... love the child when it's born. She may get away from Conway. My God, why should I feel sorry for her?'

'Yesterday ... last night you seemed ...'

'What he's doing to her is terrible, it's monstrous, but – '

'You kept crying and saying "poor girl, poor girl".'

'I was drunk, then. I feel *pity* – pity for everyone. Even Jake, now I'm here, away from him. But I'm not sorry for her. I wouldn't do a thing to help her ... All right. It's not true. How long can we sit talking here?'

'As long as you like. It's Saturday.'

'What's the time?'

'Eight o'clock.'

'Your watch must have stopped.'

'No. It's eight. Look, you've been awake all night – why don't you sleep now?'

'Saturday?'

'That's right.'

'They'll all be home. You know ... what started as a small affair of Jake's, nothing at all important, perhaps ... perhaps it wasn't important ... has grown so big, it's involved so many people – '

'I don't think it was particularly unimportant if he was busy getting her pregnant while you were being carved up like that.'

'I never said that was when it happened! I never told you that!'

'But it's pretty obvious, isn't it? Maybe he had regrets suddenly – that he'd never be a father again.'

'Don't! That's not you! It's ... Conway.'

'You said you weren't sorry for her. But it wasn't true. Well, I'm not sorry for Jake Armitage and that's the complete truth. Now what are you going to do? Stay here?'

'I behaved like Jake, you mean. But you let it happen, you didn't fight, you didn't even seem unhappy.'

'It's over, for God's sake. Are you going to stay?'

'You don't love me, do you?'

'I don't know. I haven't the ability to love you, or anyone.

I can't offer you anything, I never could. That happiness you talk about all came from you, there was this great, energetic conviction that kept us all bouncing like ping-pong balls on an air-jet. Well, now you're like this . . . what can I do? Stay here. Sleep. I'll feed you, listen to you, do what I can. But respect my inadequacy, if you don't mind. I know who I am and what I'm like. I wouldn't want you to mistake me for anyone else.'

'I don't . . .'

'Don't cry. Your Jamaican may have said that we give the gift of our love to unworthy men and women, but he didn't tell you how to get it back. You can't get it back, once it's given. All you can give the Yahwehs is a seven thousandth part of a substitute, because you feel so empty and dead, having given away so much of yourself that you must try and fool yourself that you're capable of *something*. All right. Try and fool yourself. Run about the place for a while saying you don't know who you are or what you're like or what you want. You do know. You just won't accept it. It doesn't matter, there's plenty of time.'

'No. There isn't. I can't stay, Giles.'

'Go to bed now, and sleep. Later on, I'll ring them up. I'll tell them you're here.'

'But – '

'Don't rush into anything. Just sleep. I'll ring Jake and tell him you're with me.'

'With you?'

'I'll tell him I'm looking after you. For the time being.'

23

I woke in the dark – a small bed, curiously cold air. At first, but for no more than a second, I thought I was back in the nursing home. Then I even remembered where I had put Giles's dressing-gown. I pulled it on as I got out of bed and groped towards the slit of light under the door. Giles was reading. He dropped the book on the floor and held out his hands, welcoming me.

'Did you ring them?' I asked.

'Yes. I spoke to Jake. I told him you were here. I told him not to worry. Do you know you've slept for eleven hours?'

'What did he say? Was he ...? Did he ask why? Was he ... angry?'

'No. Just worried. He thought you might have thrown yourself in the river, or something. That's what he said. He seemed very relieved to know you were here.'

'Well ... I suppose that's ... natural.' I didn't know what Jake would say under these circumstances. It seemed quite likely that it would be, 'I thought she might have thrown herself in the river, or something.' I could hear him saying it, as though I were old tea-leaves, orange peel thrown out of a passing boat. 'And the children?'

'They're all right. Dinah told them you'd gone to stay with your mother, she told them your mother was ill. She's ringing your mother to tell her she's ill. You see – it's all very simple. I lit the geyser hours ago. You can have a bath if you like. Then I'll take you out and feed you.'

'*Dinah* told them that?'

'So he said.'

'Then where does Dinah think I am?'

'She knows now. Look, children are tough. You've got a perfect right to go off if you want to. Don't worry.'

'Did he ask ... when I was going back?'

'No.'

'Well ... did he ... Didn't he ask *why*?'

'No.'

'Nothing?'

'No. I said you'd contact him when you felt ... able.'

'You mean he said *nothing*?'

'No.'

'Oh ... Can I have a drink? Are you having a drink?'

'Of course. I've been sitting here for hours, getting plastered and reading this appalling book.'

'You never used to drink.'

'Neither did you.'

'Did he sound upset, or angry, or – didn't he care?'

'Why don't you ring him yourself?'

'No – I can't.'

'Well, he can contact you any time. He's got the number and the address. It's up to him, isn't it?'

I bathed in the narrow, chipped bathtub, scoured myself with ascetic soap. I'm living my own life, God help me. I have drawn the line, gone so far and no further. Jake, Jake, what am I doing here? 'You mustn't wave to him like that! He'll think you want to see him!' 'Well, I do want to see him!' I want to fly from a window and pour through the air like a wind of love to raise his hair and slide into the palms of his hands. But it's up to him. My dear Ireen, what does it matter who it's up to? Well, if it doesn't matter to you, it doesn't matter to me, I'm sure. I'd only like to ask where it's got you, that's all – you've a very nasty scar there, dear, if you don't mind my saying so, and it's not a very pleasant thing when the only person you have to turn to after all these years is your ex. I wonder whether that baby will look like Jake, of course he's bound to see it, it'll be a bond between them for ever, Jake's youngest child ...

'You've been crying again,' Giles said. 'You should sing in the bath, not cry in it, why don't you ever do anything right? Here, have a drink.'

'I have arguments with myself.'

'About what?'

'Between the part of me that believes in things, and the part that doesn't.'

'And which wins?'

'Sometimes one. Sometimes the other.'

'Then stop arguing. Powder your nose, and we'll go out.'

When we got back to the flat after dinner, I felt sure there would be some message, some sign from Jake. There was nothing. Giles showed me his Hi-Fi – of course he had built it himself – and played records, Giles sitting with his head against my knees, his eyes closed. I believed that at any moment the doorbell or the telephone would ring. 'You're arguing,' Giles said. 'You're not tired. Come on, we'll go out.'

'We could go somewhere in the car, if you like.' I thought I might drive where I could see the lights of the house.

'No, we'll walk.'

We walked to the river, along the river, over bridges, past bright furniture shops and drapers, shut houses, pubs, churches, miles of railing, corridors of brick, streets, cross-roads. Giles talked, and I kept my legs moving one after the other, left, right, left, right, keeping in step. We went to bed and slept. Again, when I woke, it was nearly night-time. No, Giles said, no one had telephoned, no one had come. We went out to the same restaurant, but I paid for the meal. Afterwards, Giles suggested going to the pictures but I pretended that films, anything to do with films, distressed me. Instead, I bought a bottle of brandy and we went back to the flat.

'I've got no clothes, no make-up, no anything. What shall I do?'

'I'll go and get you some in the morning.'

'You can't, in the morning. You have to go to work.'

'I shan't go tomorrow.'

He didn't actually follow me about, but he watched me, he was always there. He watched me thinking. He heard my feelings. I said I could sleep in the armchair that night, but he made me go to bed and took a spare blanket from the cupboard for himself in the armchair. I felt so guilty about him, and so lonely, that after a while I got up and fetched him. He came with the same uncomplaining grace that he did everything, but in bed he suddenly burst into tears and clutched at me as though he were dreaming. I twisted my head, clenched my hands, calling for Jake again and again, amazed that my body was putting up no resistance. My skin grew no spurs, barbs, thorns, briers to protect it, I had no shell to shrink into – why, when the rest of me was speared like a battlefield? At last he cried my name out loud, and I knew that at that moment he thought he was alone. Then, slowly, the realization that I was there came back to him. There was nothing to say. We were both ashamed, both silent. He moved away from me. I said, 'I must go in the morning.'

'Yes. I know. Where will you go?'

'I don't know. Perhaps to the tower. Perhaps ... I don't know.'

He was silent for a long time. Then he got out of bed, he was standing up somewhere in the dark room. I asked whether I should put the light on.

'No. No. I've got something to tell you.'

'Well? What is it?'

He hesitated. 'I've only had two feelings in my life,' he said at last. 'Love for you ...'

'Yes?'

'And hatred. I didn't know there was such a thing. Hatred.'

'Of course there's such a thing. Why don't you turn the light on? I can't see you.'

'I hated Jake.'

'Yes.'

'You don't understand. I've only had two feelings in my life.'

'Yes, I do understand.'

'I'm empty. You, the children ... were taken by Jake. After that I was empty.'

'We weren't taken by –'

'Yes, you were!' he shouted. The sound was abrupt and violent.

'Let me turn the light on. Please.'

'No. Leave it off. Wait till I've finished ... That pitiful performance you just witnessed – God knows you couldn't take part in it – was me. Me. Myself. As I now am. Do you understand?'

'Look, you're good, Giles. You're kind. There isn't anybody like you. Just because – '

'Good? Kind?'

'It's not fair to you if I stay here. That's all.'

'You don't mean that.'

'All right. I don't want to stay.'

'We've had this conversation before.'

'Yes. What were you going to tell me?'

There was a long silence. I didn't care what he had to tell me. In the darkness I covered my face with my hands, pressing my hands against my jaw and forehead, longing to break the bone. Nothing I could do to myself would hurt enough. Everything was an indulgence, courage and cowardice, punishment and crime, honesty and deceit; everything was corrupt; nothing, no regret, remorse, no penitence was untainted by pleasure. I might as well stay with Giles, revelling in disgust; I might as well give in. Avoid evil? There's nothing else. Nothing else in my own head. Nothing else in me.

'I lied to you about Jake,' Giles said.

'What?' I looked up, over my hands, into the darkness. 'What did you say?'

'I lied to you. About Jake. He rang up ... oh, half a dozen times.'

I groped for the light, turned it on. He was naked and turned with his back to me, desperately looking about for some covering.

'What do you mean? When did he ring up? When?'

He was stumbling into his clothes. 'When you were asleep. Yesterday. Today ... Each time I told him you didn't want to talk to him ... I left the phone, as though to ask you, and went back and said you wouldn't talk to him ... I was comforting him, can you believe that? Laughing my bloody head off, *comforting* him ... Even *he* thinks I'm good, kind, self-sacrificing, poor bloody Giles only wants to help ... Well, you came back to me, didn't you? You came back to me, didn't you? You came back to me?'

'No!'

He sat down, collapsing. I dragged on my clothes, tearing them, laddering them. In the large, mahogany-framed, mildewed mirror I saw his face sagging open, as though it had been plundered. I got my coat on, tied the belt, combed my fingers through my hair.

'Good-bye, Giles.'

'You're going home? You won't find Jake there.'

I crossed the room. As I got to the door he repeated, 'Jake's not there.'

'You think I believe you?'

He leapt up and grabbed my arm. For a moment he held it tightly, then his hand dropped.

'He's gone ... to his father. He went yesterday. He's been ringing you from there.'

'He wanted me to go there?'

'Yes.'

'You told him I wouldn't go?'

'Yes.' He raised his head. The faintest shadow of pleasure, almost a smile, moved across his face. 'Anyway ... it's too late now. His father died, this morning.'

24

'Let me wither and weare out mine age in a discomfortable, in an unwholesome, in a penurious prison, and so pay my debts with my bones, and recompense the wastefulness of my youth, with the beggary of mine age. Let me wither in a spittle under sharp and foul and infamous diseases, and so recompense the wantonness of my youth with that loathsomeness in mine age; yet, if God withdraw not His spiritual blessings, His Grace, His Patience, if I can call my suffering His doing, my passion His action, all this that is temporal is but a caterpiller got into one corner of my garden, but a mill-dew fallen upon one acre of my corn. The body of all, the substance of all is safe, as long as the soul is safe. But when I shall trust to that, which we call a good spirit, and God shall deject and impoverish and evacuate that spirit; when I shall rely upon a moral constancy, and God shall shake and enfeeble and enervate, destroy and demolish that constancy; when I shall think to refresh myself in the serenity and sweet air of a good conscience, and God shall call up the damps and vapours of hell itself, and spread out a cloud of diffidence, and an impenetrable crust of desperation upon my conscience; when health shall fly from me, and I shall lay hold upon riches to succour me and comfort me in my sickness, and riches shall fly from me, and I shall snatch after favour and good opinion to comfort me in my poverty; when even this good opinion shall leave me, and calumnies and misinformations shall prevail against me; when I shall need peace, because there is none but Thou, O Lord, that should stand for me, and then shall find that all the wounds I have come from Thy hand, all the arrows that stick in me, from Thy quiver; when I shall see that because I have given myself to my corrupt nature, Thou hast changed Thine; and because I am all evil towards Thee, therefore Thou has given over being good towards me; when it comes to this height, that the fever is not in the humours, but in the spirits, that mine enemy is not an imaginary enemy, fortune, nor a transitory enemy, malice in great persons, but a real and an irresistible and an inexorable and an everlasting enemy, the Lord of Hosts Himself, the Almighty God Himself, the Almighty God Himself only knows the weight of this affliction, and except He put in that *pondus gloriae*, that exceeding weight of an eternal glory, with His own hand into the other scale, we are weighed down, we are swallowed up, irreparably, irrevocably, irrevocably, irremediably ...'

The rich, actor's voice sank into silence. The old man in his funeral clothes, his silver hair like a prophet, walked slowly down the chancel steps and stepped sideways into the front pew. After a moment's pause the Air on the G String, relayed on tape from the organ loft, sang through an uneasy silence. It gathered the noble and despairing words and suspended them in a perfect cone, a capsule of eternity, over the lonely coffin. Sitting next to Jake I was afflicted, physically afflicted in shoulder, hip and thigh, by his sense of betrayal. He was a child mocked by a father who had played games like a child and now, in death, turned gravely to adult matters, leaving him alone. His father had been the progenitor of Jake's whole world, its prime example: sceptical, tepid, suspicious of emotion, contemptuous of the laws he scrupulously kept, a member of success and an enemy of failure; if he had acknowledged conscience, he had shrugged it away; the only thing that had ever tortured him was boredom. Why had he ended his life with this agonized cry for help? The only time that Jake had spoken to me since I came, he had burst out, 'Why did he want this read? He didn't believe all that!'

I said awkwardly, 'Well ... it's beautiful.'

'Beautiful? He was a bloody liar.'

'It doesn't matter.'

'He didn't trust me.'

'He loved you,' I said uselessly.

'I thought he was like me. I honestly thought he was ... myself. Now it turns out he was quite different.'

'No.'

'I never tried to understand him. I never thought there was anything to ... understand. Just a likeable old bastard, mean with his money ... liked whisky, liked his cigars, he liked food. And his writing – it wasn't good ... professional, though. Successful. I thought he just wanted to live. What more did he want? What *more*?'

'I don't know, Jake. I don't know.'

'There isn't any more.'

But every inconsistent wish had been observed, nevertheless. The vicar, crouching back in the choir stalls, looked deeply unhappy. He was troubled by a sensation of blasphemy. The friends, five old men, only one of them with a wife, sat peacefully enjoying the music, the spring sun, the smell of lilies. When the music ended four of the old men – the actor did not go – rose and stood apprehensively at the corners of the coffin. Four burly undertakers, jostling the old men, lifted the coffin and lowered it on to the old men's fragile shoulders. A wreath slipped off the tipped end of the coffin and the vicar put his hand over his eyes in quick prayer. There was a hurried consultation among the undertakers, and swift as children picking daisies they stripped the coffin of flowers while the old men stood trembling, throwing hopeless looks up the aisle to the open door. Jake was gripping the front of the pew, leaning forward on his arms as though he were going to be sick. I could hear his father saying, 'Absolutely no good asking Jake to carry the box. He'd be sure to drop it,' – and then smiling at him, taking his hand, giving him love but never responsibility. There was nothing I could do. I was a stranger.

Finally, after some scuffling, two of the undertakers crouched under the sides of the coffin, bending low to level up with the old men, who edged uncertainly forward to the brink of the steps and then, at last, proceeded. The vicar pursued them, his face tense, his eyes half shut, waiting for the inevitable crash. But the old men stepped out bravely, although their feet hardly seemed to touch the floor and they were more suspended from the coffin than supporting it. The two undertakers breathed heavily, trying to maintain their expressions of pious gloom while bearing the yoke of an ebony coffin and five schoolfriends, one dead. Jake and I followed. The actor, the solitary wife and the housekeeper fell in behind us. We went out into the warm air. Two children playing catch among the tombstones stopped, stared at us and backed away, running when they were beyond the gate.

Jake would not go to the grave. The vicar signalled to him, but he turned his back on the deep hole, with its emerald lining that could have more usefully been used for a display of lawn mowers and garden rakes than for disguising the solid walls of a grave: the walls of earth, clay, stone, worm and root, hospitable and alive, were made indecent by that horror of fancy raffia. The old men stood perilously near the edge, peering down with the fascination of people looking into the crater of a volcano. How long before they too would jump? Their rusty black clothes were shadows, their faces peaked with fear and curiosity. I stayed with Jake, although he did not know I was there. He was alone. He no longer needed me.

The vicar, able at last to speak, bared a voice that sent the rooks cawing from the elms and made a cow, browsing the churchyard hedge, raise its head in gentle inquiry. 'Earth to earth!' he bellowed, as though he were giving judgement. 'Ashes to ashes! Dust to dust! ...' *But except he put in that exceeding weight of an eternal glory with his own hand into the other scale, we are weighed down, we are swallowed up* ... I felt diminished, lost, as unrelated to reality or purpose as a piece of cotton caught on a branch, a fragment of china in the grass. Who was I, to come to terms with evil? What arrogance. But it's arrogance that keeps one alive: the belief that one can choose, that one's choice is important, that one is responsible only to oneself. Without arrogance what would we be? I longed now to know what Jake's father had really thought, had really felt and suffered behind that bland barricade. But it was too late. He had made quite certain that the one great statement of his life would be made after his death, involving him in nothing.

I touched Jake's hand, but he didn't turn, or look up. I wanted to ask him to forgive me, as I, at that moment only, forgave him. But it was impossible. I walked slowly away across the churchyard. When I turned at the gate, and looked back, I saw the five old men with their heads bowed, standing together, and the younger man standing alone, isolated, as he had chosen.

25

I went to the tower. There, in a cell of brick and glass, I sat and watched the wall of sky that rose ten feet away from my look-out window. Nothing else existed. Nobody else lived. A thick mist packed the surrounding valleys and rain, very fine rain, fell incessantly, to obscure the world further. The birds clattered, invisible: or sometimes drifted like burnt paper across the window, were carried up and away again, lying on their wings as though half asleep.

I seemed to be alone in the world. My past, at last, was over. I had given it up; set it free; sent it back where it belonged, to fit into other people's lives. For one's past grows to a point where it is longer than one's future, and then it can become too great a burden. I had found, or had created, a neutrality between the past that I had lost and the future that I feared: an interminable hour which passed under my feet like the shadow of moving stairs, each stair recurring again and again, flattening to meet the next, a perfect circle of isolation captive between yesterday and tomorrow, between two illusions. Yesterday had never been. Tomorrow would never come. Darkness and light succeeded each other. The thick log in the grate became a heap of ash. Did this mean time continuing? I didn't believe it. The high tower, rising like a lighthouse in a sea of mist, was inaccessible to reality. Even the birds flung themselves about as though there were no trees, no earth to settle on.

I had been married for twenty-four years, more than half my life. The children who were born during my first wedding night now walked heavily about, frowning, groping in worn handbags for small change; their clothes were beginning to grow old and many of them must have stopped falling in love. I found it hard to understand this, as I found it hard to grasp the idea of distance, or as I always found it hard to believe in the actuality of other people's lives. For further proof, there were my own children, who until recently I had loved and cared for. Some were still growing up. Some merely grew thinner or fatter, but the size of their feet, the length of their arms, the circumference of their wrists and ankles would never change, except from disease. In them, in their memories and dreams, I existed firmly enough, however unrecognizable to myself. I stood over stoves, stirring food in a saucepan; I bent and picked things up from the floor; I stepped from side to side in the ritual of bed-making; I ran to the garden calling 'Rain!' and stretched up for the clothes-pegs, cramming them into one fist and hurrying in, bedouined with washing. I shook thermometers, spooned out medicine; my face hung pinkly over the bath, suspended in steam, while I scrubbed at the free, tough flesh over a knee-cap, removing stains. I glowered, frightening, and then again sagged, sank, collapsed with the unendurable labours of a Monday. All this, and more, I saw myself perform in my children's memories, but although I knew that at one time it was so, I could not recognize myself. My children could remember stories of my own childhood, although they found them boring; but I was severed even from those old, clear images which determine, as I had previously thought, everything. The images of my childhood had disappeared.

But on the hill, in the tower, there were no children to identify me or to regulate the chaos of time. It was very light, the glare of the mist more accurate than sunshine. I had taken the telephone receiver off its rest: it lay like an unformed foetus on the table, its cord twisted in thick knots. No postman, milkman, baker or grocer walked on the gravel. The sound of their footsteps, of their low gears grinding up the track, would in any case have been muffled, and I would not have known they were there until they rang the bell. But I was safe. I had ordered no milk or bread, no cornflakes, flour, butter, cocoa, cat food, assorted jellies, biscuits, bacon, honey, cake, salad cream, sugar, tea, currants, chutney, tomato ketchup, gelatine, cream of tartar, soap, detergents, salt, shoe polish, cheese, sausages, rice, baking powder, margarine, orange squash, blackcurrant syrup, tins of soup or beans or salmon, disinfectant or instant coffee. The women who came to clean, in their fitted coats and Wellington boots, with wedding rings embedded in fingers glazed and pudgy as crystallized fruit, sat home by their fires and cared for their families. Only the wild cats knew I was there. They lay upstairs, spread out on separate beds with their stomachs heaving and their feet crossed, sleeping as though they were tired.

From time to time I put another log on the fire. I was very aware of comfort. The heat in the tower made irregular, small noises: a sudden thud through the pipes, a creaking, the slow hiss as a log blistered. I sat down again by the window. A man serving a life sentence will never again have children. Capable, strong, alert to love, he stares from his tower and cannot prevent his body growing older. His body is an uninhabited house and the outside walls are the last to crumble. I was alone with myself, and we watched each other with steady, cold, inward eyes: the past and its consequence, the reality and its insubordinate dream.

*

I stayed in the tower for three days, until they came for me. Of course if I hadn't known they would come for me, I might have gone somewhere else, I suppose that's pretty obvious. I didn't think of that. My only feeling was ... I wanted to get away. Most people, I know, have this fantasy. One day they'll walk out of the door, through the garden gate, and ... then? Then what? The fact is, you don't only need money, luggage, a ticket and a plan: you need a state of mind to think of all these things, and that state of mind is the one that keeps you at home, it's not the state of mind you're in when you're running away. Of course there are people who take out their savings, arrange for ropes and ladders, leave notes on the mantelpiece, provide themselves with some elaborate disguise;

but I imagine that they are convinced that there is some preferable future. I wasn't convinced of this at all. I wanted to postpone the future; to stop things happening to me. I couldn't have gone to a bank – anyway, they'd have been closed – or collected some clothes or looked at a map; if I could, there would have been no need to go. So I went to the tower, which I knew was empty. And having got there, I stayed there. I'd run out of petrol and so I couldn't have left; that is, without a plan.

You think men don't behave like this? Perhaps it's true. A man has to be drunk, or insane, or unbalanced by talent, before he'll behave like a woman. But I have known men cry, try to pray; I've known men whose passion for triviality far exceeded mine; I've known men more weakly and willingly victimized by circumstances than I. Even love, which is believed to obsess us, can preoccupy some men to the point where they stop fighting successfully, working well, making sufficient money. You think well-adjusted, usefully occupied women don't behave like this? Of course. They haven't the time. Everyone, men, women, even children, has a great potential for fear, unhappiness, cowardice, lack of faith – but these things are unacceptable, and must be crowded out by occupation. If I had taken a job as ... what? A receptionist, a cook, a shop assistant, a woman who does surveys for soap powders? If I had done that, instead of coming to the tower, would I have been happier? All right. Possibly I would. So, possibly, would Mrs Evans, who, unlike me, was overworked. Do you remember her? I never wrote to her after all. I suppose she thought I didn't care. I'm sorry.

I wish I could say that during that time in the tower I reached some conclusions about something; that I left the tower of my own free will, having sensibly telephoned for them to bring some petrol; and went home to the children, having discovered that they were more important to me than ... But I didn't. I stayed still and I stayed alone, for the first time in my life; and I waited for Jake.

Oh, I wasn't waiting for him as you wait for a lover, for someone coming back, or someone who is going to save you from danger. I didn't expect Jake to do anything for me. I waited for him as you wait on a hill, in a tower, in the mist, for an enemy. He had already incapacitated me, harried me, cut away most of my illusions and some of my ignorance; he had already so weakened me that I was falling back on myths, words, mysteries to replace what I had lost. I knew he wouldn't leave it at that. So I waited for him. And at first I felt calm and empty, as though nothing mattered, as though the past and the future were both meaningless. Then I thought of Jake standing alone in the churchyard, with his back turned on his father's grave, and I began to feel frightened. I bolted the doors and went up to the highest room in the tower. It is all glass, this room, but it was surrounded by cloud, and I couldn't even see the ground. I opened one of the windows and looked down, but I could only see a bed of mist. To be dead would be a perfect solution for me, I thought. But I couldn't bear the idea of pain, the possibility that I would be a broken mess on the gravel, bleating for help. I used to be physically very brave, but now if I pricked my finger I couldn't look at it. I shut the window and went downstairs again. It began to get dark. I wondered whether he would come up the hill in the night, when I couldn't see him, or in the day, when the mist would muffle the sound of his footsteps.

These were the last hours in which I loved Jake as I had loved him since the night when I took all Philpot's possessions and dumped them in the garden. How long ago was that ... nine years? These were the last hours of being joined to him by fear, and anger, and sexual necessity. This was the last time that I demanded – of him? of what? – that he should change, even secretly, as his father had changed; the last time I believed it to be possible. You don't know Jake. You only know me. Therefore it probably seems absurd to you that I ever expected so much of a man who must seem to you very normal, limited, understandable, a man who as far as you can see did his best, after all. To Jake, living is necessarily defective, vicious, care-less, an inevitable time of activity between two deaths; to him the world is a little spinning piece of grit on which sad and lonely human beings huddle together for warmth, sentimental but unfeeling, always optimistic, but embarrassed by any real hope. That is the basis on which he works, and loves, and will eventually die. It's enough for him. Those were the last hours – that night, when I was waiting – during which I tried to believe that it was Jake who was deluded and I ... It's amazing how vanity clings on to the very end, you open your dead eyes to look in the mirror which they are holding to your mouth. I still believed I was right. I was still on about avoiding evil; avoiding the messes in the street, the dust, the cruelty in one's own nature, the contamination of others. I still believed that with the slightest effort we could escape to some safe place where everything would be ordered and good and indestructible, where Simpkin and Conway could never threaten us: a place where we could trust the trees not to fall down and crush us, the birds not to peck us to death, the earth not to split open under our feet. This belief wasn't strong any more, but it still clung to me, tried to comfort me through the night. I was convinced by now that it wasn't true. Jake's battle was as good as won, if only he'd known it.

But he didn't. I sat by the window in the morning, looking out. The mist had cleared a little, like an outgoing tide, and the peak of the hill, on which the tower stood, was free of it. The garden – what would one day be the garden – sloped down to the brow of the hill and against that the mist lay just as thickly as on the previous days. There was no hedge or fence dividing us from the field below. I looked straight into the mist, which dazzled me.

They came up over the brow of the hill spread out, like beaters. In the first second I saw only one child; then they rose up from every part of the small horizon, advancing through the mist, breaking it down, coming slowly on up the stony hill with their heads lowered and their short, strong legs moving like pistons. I must hide, I thought – hide. Where? Through the back door, then? Hide in the scrub and then ... ? But they were fanning out; some were taking the back path; they were surrounding me. Where's Jake? I thought it would be Jake who would come. I could hear them now, coming across the gravel. I ran to the bottom of the stairs, where there were no windows; I ran up the spiral stairs, two at a time, and into the high, top room. They were swarming round the tower, trying the doors.

'There's no point in waiting for the key, you fool. It's bolted.'

'Let's try the window, then. There's bound to be a window.'

I had been waiting for Jake. I could have bargained with him. I could have made some effort to defend myself, however useless. But what could I do against my children? Tell them to go away, leave me alone? Oh clever Jake, wily Jake ... 'For God's sake,' I said out loud, 'they're breaking in ...'

There was a splintering crash and a high, cold voice said, 'Now you've done it.'

'Are you all right?'

'I say – he's broken the window.'

A voice from inside the house said, 'Hang on a tick, I'll unbolt the door.' I began to laugh; I laughed with the back of my wrist against my mouth, trying to stifle and control the laughter that was attacking me from inside myself.

'Well, where is she?'

'She's probably still in bed.'

'I'm going to find the cats.'

Some of them were already half-way up the stairs. They stopped, and looked up at me; I was still laughing, but they didn't ask me why. I looked at each one, and finally at Dinah. She smiled.

'Well ...' I said. 'How did *you* get here?'

'He stopped in the village. He told us to come first.'

'But ... all of you? Where's Josephine?'

They glanced at each other. Some clapped their hands over their mouths and made great eyes. The older ones turned to Dinah. 'She left,' Dinah said.

'Left? When?'

'On Wednesday.'

'But ... why?'

'She said she couldn't go on.'

'Then who's been ... looking after you?'

'Dinah didn't go to school.'

'We managed all right.'

I went down the stairs. They stood back to let me pass, then raced on up the stairs, from room to room, calling the cats.

'He said we should come here,' Dinah said.

'Yes. Of course.'

I went outside. The air was much warmer than I had expected.

'He's buying some bread and stuff,' Dinah said. 'In case you haven't got any.'

I saw Jake climbing up through the mist. Clear of it, he stopped, looked up at the tower, then came on. I was no longer frightened of him. I no longer needed him. I accepted him at last, because he was inevitable.

'I brought the children down,' he said. 'I thought I might join you for a while.'

I have tried to be honest with you, although I suppose that you would really have been more interested in my not being honest. Some of these things happened, and some were dreams. They are all true, as I understood truth. They are all real, as I understood reality.